W9-BQZ-592

# JOSH BAXTER LEVELS UP

Press Start

# JOSH BAXTER LEVELS UP

WRITTEN BY
## GAVIN BROWN

Scholastic Press
New York

Library of Congress Cataloging-in-Publication Data

Brown, Gavin 1983– author.
Josh Baxter levels up / by Gavin Brown.—First edition.
pages cm
Summary: Because his family has moved again, Josh Baxter is starting at a new school for the third time in two
years, and this time he has really started off on the wrong foot—but when his mother takes away the video games that
have become his refuge because of his poor grades, Josh realizes he has to come up with a new strategy for success.
ISBN 978-0-545-77294-5
1. Moving, Household—Juvenile fiction. 2. Middle schools—Juvenile fiction. 3. Families—Juvenile fiction.
4. Video games—Juvenile fiction. 5. Bullying—Juvenile fiction. [1. Moving, Household—Fiction. 2. Middle schools—Fiction.
3. Schools—Fiction. 4. Family life—Fiction. 5. Video games—Fiction. 6. Bullying—Fiction.] I. Title.
PZ7.1.B795Jo 2016
813.6—dc23
[Fic]
2015016236

10 9 8 7 6 5 4 3 2 1     16 17 18 19 20

Printed in the U.S.A.   23

First edition, March 2016

Book design by Christopher Stengel

For Mom and Dad, who may have been baffled by my love of games, but never once stopped supporting me.

# Table of Contents

# THAT NEW GAME SMELL

The school bus is a loading screen for my new life, the empty space in a video game between challenges. I sit by the window, wondering what's on the next level and watching the other kids get on the bus. My new classmates are wearing the kinds of clothes I thought only people on TV wore, back before we moved to a big-city suburb.

Mom said I couldn't bring my handheld on the first day of school, because I should make friends and not "be glued to that thing the whole day." So I spend the ride imagining myself running along beside the bus, backflipping over the road signs and vaulting over mailboxes. The landscape I'm Mario-ing my way through is home, at least for now. New town, new house, new school. And no player's guide to give me the tips and tricks I need to make it through the year. This is one game I have to figure out how to beat on my own.

Mom says she was lucky that a job offer came in as the company went under. It doesn't feel so lucky to me, having to move *again* during what should have been the first week of school. So for the third time in two years, I'm the new kid. This time, my sister Lindsay and I are showing up after everyone has already settled in.

The bus pulls into the school parking lot and I see the next challenge that Mom's forced on me. Howard Taft Middle School, three times the size of any of my old schools. Gym, classrooms, science labs, auditorium, library—and three hundred kids in my grade. I stand up with the other kids and shuffle forward as my heart starts banging like the drum track for a boss battle.

The loading screen is over. It's game on.

Yesterday afternoon I came to school, met with the guidance counselor, and got my class schedule, a map, and a flier about school spirit. As starting inventories go, it's pretty pathetic. Couldn't I at least get a rusty sword or a mysterious ancient artifact?

Before I know it I'm staring into the depths of my locker: Vault 151. Base of operations. Today my vault holds only the books, pencils, and binders that I brought with me—but with the right gear, an adventurer can accomplish anything. I close the door. I'll just have to find grappling hooks, spell scrolls, and health potions along the way. Or maybe an enchanted hammer. I'm not picky.

I take three steps down the hallway before I realize I've forgotten one key thing: Vault Security. A total noob mistake. I go back and pull out my shiny new lock.

As it clicks shut, someone taps me on the shoulder. I turn around. The girl is a punk princess, with streaks of blue in her hair and a black outfit with more flaps and rivets than I can count. Back in my old school, the only thing that distinguished groups of kids was whether your shirt was of a band, a sports team, or a video game. Between this girl and the kids on the bus, I can't be more out of my element with my messy brown hair that hasn't been cut since ancient times, my thick-rimmed glasses, and my favorite T-shirt— Link from Legend of Zelda holding his bow and leading Robin Hood's merry men out of Sherwood Forest. Even the shirt, as much as I love it, is starting to get too small.

"Hi, I'm Maya," she says.

"Um, hi, I'm Josh," I answer. A couple of her friends are watching from down the hall.

She points at my lock. "I . . . think you just put your lock on my locker."

"No, this is mine, it's 151."

She raises an eyebrow and points to the number above the locker that I've bolted shut: 153. I feel like even more of a noob than before. In my rush to secure the vault, I've snapped my lock on the wrong door.

I grab the lock with my left hand and stare at it. The other day I committed the combination to memory and destroyed the paper, secret agent style.

"I, uh . . ." My brain shuts down, like a glitchy game that freezes just before a crucial moment.

If only I had the ability to figure out the combination by listening as I spun the dial, or casting an opening spell. But that takes years of wizard school, and all I've learned in the last couple years are the key dates of the Revolutionary War and how to reduce fractions and—

The bell rings. I glance at the Punk Princess.

"Seriously? You forgot the combination?" Maya rolls her eyes.

"I don't know . . . should we . . ." My voice trails off.

"Great, now I'm going to be late." Maya sighs. "Wait here."

 As she walks away, I notice that her backpack has a patch with a punk Princess Daisy on it. I want to say how cool it is, but what's the point? She already hates me.

Kids head to their homerooms and the hallways empty out. Maya comes back with the guidance counselor, Mr. Alpert, in tow. Mom and I met with him yesterday for my quick orientation. He has platinum blond hair and pale skin, and is about nine feet tall. Or something. I'm not so good at estimating the height of things that high up. I can't help thinking he's some kind of frost giant trying to pass as a human.

"Don't worry, Josh, the janitor's coming to cut it off," Mr. Alpert says. "I was looking for you anyway, to make sure you got to your first class." For a huge guy, he has this tiny, tiny voice, like he's afraid if he speaks too loudly he'll break something. And I can see why he had a hard time finding me—we must all look like ants to him.

I keep looking down at my sneakers, hoping that this will all be over soon.

"How are you holding up?" he asks. "I know how socially challenging first days of school can be."

"Fine, I guess, except . . ." I gesture at the lock.

"Adjusting to a new environment can be emotionally trying," Mr. Alpert says. "I want you to feel like you can share anything with me."

"Yeah, okay," I lie. "I'll do that." Maya is looking the other way and pretending not to listen, but I'm certain she hears every word.

The janitor saunters up, holding what looks like a pair of hedge clippers. He points them at my lock. "This the one?"

Mr. Alpert nods.

With a grunt, the janitor squeezes on the clippers and the lock comes off, the ring chopped in half. Maya puts away her backpack and a bunch of notebooks and supplies, locks her locker, and walks off without a word.

I take out my gym gear and triple-check that I'm actually at Vault 151 before I use the lock I brought for gym class to secure it.

"Don't worry about this, Josh. Being at a new school is mentally stressful for anyone, and it's easy to make mistakes," Mr. Alpert says, going on to tell me that soon I will have lots of friends and be totally adjusted. I nod and say "uh-huh" periodically.

Homeroom is almost over, so Mr. Alpert walks me to gym class. When we get to the door of the gym, the Frost Giant finally goes off to find someone else to embarrass.

I'm so early for gym class that the locker room is totally empty. I store my normal clothes in one of the gym lockers but have to leave it unlocked. I bring one of my notebooks with me into the gym, sit on the bleachers, and draw a sketch of Luigi dunking a basketball. I look up only when I hear people arriving.

My spider-sense is tingling. Something strange is going on. Girls are walking out of the boys' locker room, on the left. A boy is coming out of the girls' locker room, on the right. I stand up and walk over. There are small plaques next to each door and I realize what a royal goof I've made.

I assumed that the gym was laid out the same as the one in my old school, which means I left my school clothes in the girls' locker room . . . with all the girls. I want to give up on my clothes and leave them there forever, but then I'll be stuck in sweaty gym clothes for the rest of the day.

Sometimes, when faced with an impossible problem, I try to think of what my heroes would do in my situation.

**MARIO** would charge into the girls' locker room and start hitting things with his head until clothes fell out of the ceiling.

*Strategic Assessment: Unlikely to work. Also, I can't jump that high.*

**STEVE THE MINECRAFT GUY** would punch the gym floor to get a bunch of wood and make some tools, then build a tunnel into the girls' locker room so that no one could see him.

**Strategic Assessment:** *The gym floor looks pretty sturdy.*

**MEGA MAN** solves problems by jumping around and shooting plasma from his Mega Buster until he gets where he needs to be.

**Strategic Assessment:** *Didn't get the fireball-shooting gloves that I wanted for my birthday two years ago. Maybe Target has them?*

I hear a voice behind me. "Yeah, that new kid is standing there staring into the girls' locker room," some guy is saying. "What a total creep."

I spin around, heart hammering like crazy. This is how rumors get started. How lives get ruined.

"No, I was just, uh, I left my clothes in there . . ."

The guy has a grin of pure evil on his face. "So you were taking off your clothes in there?" Turning to some girls, he says, "I told you—total creep."

They giggle and follow him as he struts off. I stand there gaping.

Maya and one of her friends stay behind. Maya rolls her eyes. "I saw some boys' clothes in one of the lockers. I was wondering who left it unlocked. You're an idiot, Josh. It was the top left corner, right?"

I nod.

"Hold on," she says with a sigh.

"Watch out for Mittens," Maya's friend says while we wait. "He's a big deal around here because he's the receiver on the football team." She spits out the words so quickly I feel like I'm going to get whiplash from trying to take them all in. "They all say that with him we'll finally beat Lancaster this year. Whoever that is. I think it's a team? Football is weird. I don't really get it. I'm Taniko by the way be careful okay don't get yourself hurt."

Maya comes out a few seconds later and tosses my clothes at me. "Just ask someone to help you next time," she says, and walks off, muttering under her breath about stupid boys.

She's not wrong.

The gym teacher yells for everyone to get on the bleachers, so I rush into the boys' side, stuff my clothes into an empty locker, and run back out to join the rest of the class.

"Welcome to gym class! Let's get this train started!" the teacher bellows. He's a typical gym teacher: a body like a flabby tank and a voice so loud he practically breathes fire. I pick my notebook back up and start sketching him as a dragon, but one that's eaten so many unlucky adventurers that its wings aren't big enough to lift it off the ground anymore.

"Attendance time! Sound off when I read your name!"

He launches into the list, stumbling badly on any name that isn't Paul Smith or Amy Jones. He absolutely mangles "Maya Granados."

"May-yeah Grenade-Os!" is basically how it comes out.

"It's Maya Granados," Maya answers, in a voice that makes it clear this is not the first time she's tried to correct him.

"Right, Grenade-Os!" he shouts. A couple of the jocks snicker, and one even mimes throwing a grenade and making a surprised face.

When Mr. Barrington reads off the name "Henry Schmittendorf," it's my turn to snicker. A couple people give me weird looks. No one else even cracks a smile at the name.

The kid who made fun of me at the lockers raises his hand and says, "Here." And then Henry "Mittens" Schmittendorf glares over at me.

"You think my name is funny, Creep?" Schmittendorf hisses. He stares me down with a you are a loser and I will crush-your-life look in his eyes. I sit back hard and any urge to laugh disappears.

"Okay, kids!" Mr. Barrington says. "This week we will be playing volleyball! Divide yourselves into teams of five!"

I get up from the bleachers like a hermit crab inching out of its shell. I take a few steps down, and collide with Schmittendorf. He's like a brick wall—five inches taller than me with a lean frame, approximately ninety-nine point eight percent muscle. I tumble to the wooden floor.

"Oops, sorry," he says as he pulls me up. Then he leans in and pats me on the back like he's encouraging a teammate. While I'm choking on his horrible breath, he whispers, "I could destroy your life, Baxter. Watch yourself."

He turns away.

I laugh.

Not because I think it's funny. I don't. I'm more scared than the time I dropped my PlayStation down the stairs. Just like then, I can see a bleak life of sorrow and regret stretching out before me.

No, I laugh because I'm nervous and scared. It's a thing I do sometimes—my brain freezes and out comes a weird high-pitched laugh.

Mittens spins on his heel. Everyone in the class is staring now, and I realize what it looks like. It looks like Mittens threatened me . . . and I laughed at him.

He stares me down, eyes black with pure evil and fists  that look like they could punch out all my hit points in a single blow. My chest feels like I lost a few already from our collision. How am I going to survive this day, let alone this year?

Sometimes when you're starting out in an adventure game, there are places you just don't go, enemies you just don't want to tangle with. You're a noob with a dream and a bow made of twine and a twig. And if you step into the wrong area, poke the wrong enemy . . .

"I warned you, Creep," Mittens says, loud enough that

the kids standing around us can all hear. "You can't say I didn't warn you."

I shrivel from Schmittendorf's gaze, staring at the floor and wishing I could hit "reset," "new game," even "power off"—anything to not be here right now. The only reason Mittens doesn't deck me then and there is that Mr. Barrington shoves a ball into his hand and points him and his friends toward one of the volleyball nets.

I'm grateful that in volleyball the teams are separated by a net. If not, based on the looks Mittens is giving me, I would be on my way to the hospital by now.

Which might have been a mercy, since then I wouldn't have to go to math class.

As it is, I barely make it out of the Gymnasium of Despair alive. Mr. Barrington blows the final whistle, and it feels like I've limped out of a battle with one hit point remaining. I take a minute to lean against the wall and catch my breath. The last thing I want is to face Schmittendorf and his friends alone in the locker room.

I find my way to math class and my jaw clenches when I see Mittens sitting in the back. He looks over and flashes me a grin that comes straight from the evil that grips his soul. I wonder for a moment if there's a decent human being trapped in there, one who's been corrupted by a cursed artifact. Probably not.

I sit as far from him as I can, throwing myself into the chair so hard it hurts. I pull out my sketchbook and start drawing Mittens on a tiny raft, getting sucked into a giant toilet whirlpool of death.

"Hey, man," someone says, and I look up to see two kids. The one talking is tall and pale and wearing a Final Fantasy T-shirt. He has messy black hair and a slightly scruffy look—probably a rogue of some sort.

"Hey," I say back. You have to be careful with rogues— if I've learned one thing, it's that they'll stab you in the back the moment it's to their advantage.

"I'm Peter, and this is Chen Sheng," Peter says. His friend is short, slightly round, and wearing the kind of glasses that are geeky—not in a cool way, but more like a my-parents-bought-the-cheapest-glasses-on-the-rack way. But there's a fierce intelligence in his eyes—I wouldn't want to cross him. He'd probably start flinging fireballs and light-ning bolts at me, or cast a spell that tied my shoelaces together.

"I'm Josh," I answer.

"Hey," Chen says softly.

"So," Peter says, eyeing my notebook. "Saw you draw-ing in gym. What are you sketching in there?"

I look down at my sketch and my stomach turns to ice. I'm pretty decent at faces, and it's obviously a picture of Mittens. Peter has to have seen it, and I know exactly what would happen if Mittens knew about it. As if I'm not already in deep enough trouble.

"Listen, I know what you're trying to start," I say. "Just leave it."

"Huh? What are you talking about, man?" Peter asks.

What's he really after? My brain short-circuits and orders Nervous Laugh Protocol, betraying me for the second time in one day.

"All right, whatever," Peter says as he shrugs and turns away. Chen Sheng just looks at me with an expression of confusion, then turns and follows his friend.

They sit down a few desks away from me and start planning their strategies for something called a "decathlon." They're not making fun of me. Maybe I've made yet another boneheaded move.

As the teacher walks in and takes off his coat, a paper airplane knocks into the back of my head and lands on the floor next to me. I look down. The word *Creep* is written in big letters on the side. I don't even bother to look back—the quiet hyena laughs coming from behind me are all that I need to hear.

I put my head down on the desk as I feel  my life ending.

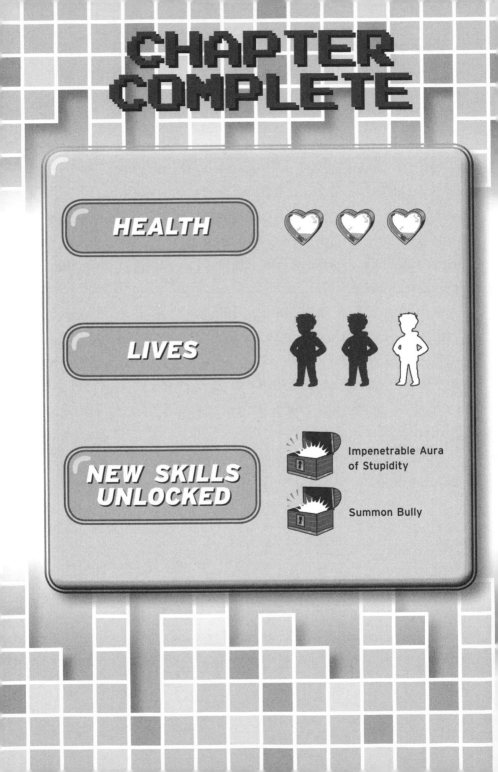

# GREEN WARRIOR NEEDS GRADES BADLY

"Did you have a good day, Joshie?" Mom asks, poking her head into my room when she gets home. I'm slouched down on my bed, holding a controller in my hand, but I haven't even been able to muster the energy to decide which game to start.

"Whatever," I say. This whole moving thing was her idea. Why shouldn't she see what it's putting me through?

"Do you want to talk about it?" she asks.

Video games are supposed to be a mom-free zone. Who would want an annoying mom asking how your day was in a game? She's like the updates that apps are constantly begging for. Necessary, sure. Important, even. But so frustrating.

I shrug. When Dad was here, at least he got my gamer needs. Even if he would sometimes take the controller to "show you one thing" and keep it for about an hour.

"Okay, well, I'll be around if you want to talk," she says, and leaves me alone.

I sit there without moving for a few more minutes. I've lost a life. But any decent game gives you at least three lives, so I have two left.

I need a plan.

While a lot of my heroes seem to punch their way out of problems, that isn't an option for me. I've never heard of someone punching their way into getting good grades or making friends. And fighting a football star, even if he deserves it, is a recipe to end up in the hospital. Football wasn't a big deal at my old schools, but down here it's more popular than an all-you-can-eat buffet. There are posters all over the halls for the big game that's coming up against Lancaster.

Mittens is tough—too tough. If I can't win with strength, my best bet is to follow the way of the ninja. Use stealth and cleverness. I figure that if no one notices what I'm doing, everything in my life will be smooth. Given how I've started out, I need to lie low for a while.

I hope that Schmittendorf will ignore me the next day, but instead he swaggers over to sneer at me in the locker room.

"Hey, Creep, seen anything good in the girls' locker room today? I bet you could fit through the air duct to sneak in there." His friends all laugh.

 The label sticks, but I ignore it. Ninjas don't react when people make fun of them.

"Eyes to yourself, Creep," Schmittendorf says every day as we pass in the hallway.

Each morning I use my ninja stealth skills to slip out of homeroom and head straight for the gym. I change clothes like it's a SpeedRun and get out of there before more than one or two guys have even arrived. And I triple-check every time that I'm going into the right locker room.

One day in math class, Mittens is telling a bunch of kids at the front of the room about some new play his team is running. I do my best to ignore him, sitting in the back drawing the giant Mitten Monster, with a diagram showing his weak points—like the membrane between the thumb and index finger—and strategic notes.

"Hey, Creep, what's your problem?" Mittens calls from the front of the classroom. I keep drawing, not even looking up. A ninja wouldn't give him the satisfaction.

"Mittens, explain about the flip-six play again," that Peter kid I talked to on the first day says. It sounds sarcastic to me, but Mittens isn't about to miss a chance to brag some more. He goes back to talking about football without me ever having to respond at all. Ninja victory.

"Students, pay attention," Mr. Ramirez says, and the room quiets down. He starts sketching something out on the board. "Today we'll learn about the surface area of regular solids."

I try to copy the symbols down onto my sheet. He's drawn a pyramid on the board, but somehow mine comes out looking more like a lopsided airplane.

"This is a regular pyramid. It's like a triangle, but in three dimensions." He speaks with excitement, as if this is somehow fun. The day before, I overheard some of the kids saying he used to be some kind of math prodigy when he was a kid. All that math must have fried his brain. I guess math is a bit like dark sorcery—even as you make use of it, it is also using you.

"Can any of you explain what a regular polyhedron is?" he asks.

One of my ninja tricks is to raise my hand even when I don't know the answer. Then I lower it, erase something, and shake my head, like I found a mistake. It makes it seem like I'm working hard and mostly understand what's going on. There's no way Mr. Ramirez will call on me after a performance like that.

And this time, at least, it works. He calls on one of the girls sitting by the windows.

Mr. Ramirez continues the lesson, ramping up the challenge as he goes. At first it all makes sense, but by the end of class it's about as easy to understand as that time I accidentally set a game to Russian mode. But I am a ninja, using stealth to avoid the world. So I nod and try to look like I get it.

Ninjas don't ask questions, no matter how confused they are.

Mr. Ramirez puts another incomprehensible problem on the board.

"Oh, I know this one! I know this one!" Taniko says to herself as she writes with one hand and raises her other hand, waving it around like a war banner. My other trick:

sit next to Taniko. She's a pure elemental force, a whirlwind trapped in the body of a girl. With her making noise and waving her hand like a maniac, I escape notice. Ninjas use the environment around them to their advantage.

"Joshua, what did you get for it? Twelve times X, right?" she whispers, as Mr. Ramirez waits for everyone to finish.

Taniko is one of the only people in the class who doesn't call me Creep. But it isn't that she wants to be nice; it's because she and Maya aren't friends with the popular kids, so they aren't plugged in to the Humiliating Nickname Update Network that lets everyone know how to ruin your life.

"Yeah," I say with a shrug, erasing my answer and writing $12x$ down on my sheet.

When the class is over and I'm walking to the door, I feel a push from behind me.

"Whoops!" Mittens says. "Sorry, Josh!" It almost sounds sincere.

My textbooks tumble out of my arms, and my sketch-book falls to the floor. Mittens leans down and picks it up, pretending to be helpful.

"Really sorry about that, man," he adds, then stops short.

I look down and it feels like my kart has been hit dead-on by a blue shell. The sketchbook is open to a picture of the Mitten Monster in all its Mitten-y glory.

Schmittendorf leans in, hissing his words like a basilisk. "You don't learn, do you? Kids used to make fun of me, used to joke about my name. No one does that anymore. And you're not going to start it, Creep."

Sometimes the universe sets you up in a conversation where there's something that just has to be said. Who am I to say no, when the powers of the universe force such a destiny on me? Usually it's a bad joke that makes my sister hit me, but sometimes . . . it gets me into big trouble.

"Yeah, must be really tough, having people make fun of you," I shoot back.

He doesn't hit me, but I can see in his eyes pure rage, the boiling suns of a villain who has marked you for utter destruction. But Mr. Ramirez is standing across the room, creating that mysterious field in which even Darth Mittens has to pretend not to have fallen completely to the dark side.

I grab my books and practically sprint to English. A few minutes later I settle into my seat, incredibly grateful that this class does *not* include Mittens.

Not getting called on in class is the best way to avoid other kids paying attention to you. But avoiding getting noticed in English class is a challenge. Mr. Ramirez in math is easy to fool, but Ms. Pritchard has the eyes of a seer, able to tell the future from tea leaves or divine the fact that you didn't do your writing homework from the guilty expression on your face.

She takes one look at me as she walks by and can instantly tell that I forgot to write my journal entries on *Tuck Everlasting.*

"Um, let me look for it," I say, rummaging through my backpack.

She doesn't even stand and wait, or pretend to believe me. You can't fool an enchantress.

"Don't try to deceive me, Josh," she says with an air of serene calm. "It demeans you and me both."

My shoulders slump. What am I going to do, argue with her when I really haven't done the reading or written my journal entry? And worst of all, I actually feel a little guilty.

Ninjas aren't supposed to feel guilt. They're supposed to be tireless, stealthy killing machines. I sit through the class and resolve to try to at least do a bit of my homework next time, so I have something to hand in. If nothing else, on the ride to school I can read the first few pages and scribble something down. Then I can avoid Ms. Pritchard's dressing down while still doing the minimum amount of effort, ninja style.

There's one important difference I'm discovering between me and ninjas: Ninjas don't have to sit through lunch at Howard Taft Middle School every single day. Do ninjas even eat? If they do, it's not sitting at a table alone or, worse, stuck with a bunch of kids who ignore them.

I'm sitting by myself when Maya and Taniko come and sit at the other end of the table.

"Oh, hello, Joshua," Taniko says. Her fingers are twirling a pen with the speed of the whirlwind. I can only imagine the endless hours of practice that have perfected that skill.

"Hey, Josh," Maya adds.

It's embarrassing to admit, but even that little bit of acknowledgment feels pretty good.

"Hey," I answer.

They sit down, and I try to pay attention to my food.

"It's weird, having Mr. Ramirez come over to my house. He and my dad are planning the Video Game Decathlon," Taniko says. I can't help but perk up.

"What's that?" I blurt out.

"Oh, it's a fund-raiser for the class trip in the spring," Maya says, offhand. She pokes her fork at Taniko. "Are you going to join our team this year?"

Taniko shrugs. "I guess so."

"We need you," Maya says, shaking her head in a way that makes me suspect this conversation has happened more than one time. "You always crush me at Mario Kart. It's too bad the Shultz sisters went to private school." She stares into the distance. "They were unstoppable at Smash Bros. With them we might have had a chance against the jock squad. Even if we get crushed at Splatoon and whatever that football game is."

Smash Bros. is my game, the one I always come back to when I finish another game or want something familiar. I've invented my own Ultimate World Championship mode where I have to win ten brawls in a row at top difficulty. I play as Luigi, and I am unstoppable.

I open my mouth to say something, but the Mitten Monster and his mitten minions are sitting down at the next table over. As he puts his tray down, Schmittendorf looks over at me. I look down at my plate, trying to avoid his gaze. My mouth is still open, so I try to cover by shoveling a spoonful of corn into it.

Maya gives me an odd look. One of those you-are-a-total-weirdo looks.

"Did you think any more about the designs for our game that I sent last week?" Maya asks Taniko, and the moment is over.

I stare into the distance, letting the pure discipline of the ninja settle over me. I'm fine. Ninjas don't need to ask questions anyway. They figure things out by intuition and silent observation. Or by demanding answers in a husky voice with a cool accent.

That afternoon when I get home, I console myself with a round of Smash Bros. Ultimate World Championship mode, to prove that I can still win at something. I'm at the end of a hard-fought ninth match when Lindsay walks in.

"How was your day?" she asks, totally interrupting my Intense Gamer Flow State. No matter how many times I explain it to her and Mom, they don't seem to get how important it is.

On-screen, Luigi falls down into oblivion, and I look up at my annoying sister. Part of why I lost my concentration is that she doesn't usually ask questions like that. I figure Mom must have asked her to check up on me.

"Fine," I answer.

Mom used to make me go outside, but with her second job at the cell phone store, she rarely makes it home for dinner. Usually Lindsay and I microwave some FastNLean meals and watch *Celebrity Yodeling Weight Loss Challenge*, or whatever show it is she insists on.

"School good?" Lindsay asks.

"Yeah, fine." I really don't want to, but I ask anyway. "You?"

That one word is all the opening she needs. She launches into some story about a boy and one of her teammates, and them only having one spoon for ice cream on their date.

I don't really listen; I just watch her hands gesture wildly as she tells the story. The movements are fascinating, like she's trying to cast some sort of gossip spell.

It gets even worse when she tries to help me.

"Josh, you should get out more," Lindsay says. She's putting on her shoes before going out to a movie with some  of her teammates. At this point I've switched to playing Star Fox and am starting to feel myself slipping into Intense Gamer Flow State, but Lindsay never lets that get in the way of harassing me.

Of course I'd be happy to be going out to a movie with some friends, but I'll let myself be tossed into Tartarus before I'll admit that to my big sister.

"I'm fine," I say, trying to keep my concentration as I navigate Fox through an asteroid field.

"No, really, why don't you go out with your friends more?"

"I'm fine, Linds. Let me play."

"Whatever." She shrugs and leaves me in peace.

I mash a button angrily and careen into the nearest asteroid. I want to yell, tell her that three new schools in two years have lost me every friend I had. Plus, last Christmas they all got the new PlayStation and now I can't even play the new games they're into. The clans we were all in have become digital ghost towns. Like my social life. Nowadays, the only contact I have with them is when they send me a picture of one of them snarfing milk in the cafeteria or whatever.

I could rage at Lindsay for the rest of the night, but I let her toxic sisterliness wash past me. With the way of the ninja, I have a secret weapon. Nothing can touch me.

# CHAPTER 3

# IT'S SUPER INEFFECTIVE!

Schmittendorf is sneering at me again. I can see the big red B+ written at the top of his math test. Which wouldn't be a big deal, except that mine is stamped with a D–. With all the homework assignments I've missed, the Pythagorean Theorem Boss Fight has not gone well.

"Let's talk after class, Josh," Mr. Ramirez says as he walks past me to pass back the rest of the tests.

Out of the corner of my eye, I can see Schmittendorf snickering. I consider using a grappling hook to climb into the ceiling tiles so I can disappear into the air vents, never to return. But ninja moves like that are hard to pull off under fluorescent school light without anyone noticing. Ninjas are much better off in a misty twilight atmosphere.

After class, Mittens swaggers out with his friends, and I stay behind to talk to Mr. Ramirez. I walk up to his desk and he looks up at me from under his spectacles, his forehead wrinkled in thought. I wait uneasily, trying my best to be patient. Ninjas don't volunteer to start difficult conversations.

Avoiding uncomfortable talks with your teachers must be a core skill all ninjas learn in ninja school.

Urgent question: Why couldn't Mom have gotten a new job somewhere that had a ninja school?

"Josh, you are close to failing grades," he says finally.

I nod. "Yeah."

"Why do you think that is?"

"I'm not very good at math, I guess," I say.

"I'm not sure that's true. You did fairly well on the placement exam. But you don't seem to be keeping up with the homework."

Math skills run in the family, with Mom being an accountant and all. She used to help me out with my math assignments, but somehow she never seems to have time for that anymore.

"I'm . . . a little distracted," I say.

Mr. Ramirez nods. "I understand. You're not actually failing at the moment. Please try to do more of your homework assignments, all right?"

"Sure," I say.

"Are you adjusting to the new school okay?" he asks.

"Yeah, I'm fine."

We look at each other silently for a moment.

"Okay, see you tomorrow," he says, turning down to the papers on his desk. "Let me know if you need any help."

The next day, when I arrive for my writing conference with Ms. Pritchard, I expect the worst. I poke my head in the door and am relieved to find her still talking with Maya. Maybe things are running behind and she won't have much time for me.

"Josh, come in and sit down," Ms. Pritchard says, smiling.

I sit. Ms. Pritchard is definitely some sort of enchantress. The fluorescent lights are off, so the light comes from lamps positioned around the room. Every wall is covered in bookshelves, and Ms. Pritchard's desk is heaped with even more books. Maya is looking at the Enchantress's piles of ancient tomes, at the posters of old authors on the walls, anywhere but at me.

"Josh, when we do writing exercises in class, you are extremely creative and prolific. But on the rare occasions that you hand in your homework, it looks like it was scribbled by a chimpanzee during an earthquake." Ms. Pritchard peers at me over the rims of her glasses. "Why do you think that is?"

Whenever I see Ms. Pritchard outside of her room, she looks out of place. Something about the round glasses, vintage clothes, and air of being slightly lost makes you want to stop her and ask if she needs directions back to her room. Or ask if you can hire her to cast a hex on a bully.

Today she looks kind of sad but determined as she waits for my answer.

I sag in my chair. "Am I failing this class, too?"

Ms. Pritchard smiles and shakes her head. "No, I'm sure you won't actually fail. But my job isn't to get you to pass with a C average. My job is to sow the seeds of creativity and have every student's sapling of knowledge grow up to his or her mighty oak of potential."

Yep, there she goes again. Taking me seriously. I glance over at Maya to see if she agrees. She is watching me with an almost nervous look on her face.

"Okay," I agree tentatively, not sure where this is going.

"You're so creative, Josh, I want to help you unlock that portion of your mind. So we're going to give you a writing tutor. Think of her like the key to open that door." She motions at Maya. "Maya is in my creative writing workshop elective, and as part of the elective, every writer must tutor a student from one of my other classes."

I gulp. I'm going to have a writing tutor? And worse, one in the same grade as me?

I want to argue, but then I glance over at Maya. She's looking at me hopefully, expectantly. And yeah, maybe there's a little pity in there, too. That part burns.

But saying no would make it seem like I want to avoid her. This is the first time since my first day when I locked my stuff in her locker that she doesn't look vaguely annoyed with me. And at this point I've made more than enough enemies.

"That, uh, sounds really great," I say.

And instantly regret it. All of my ninja strategies have landed me here: getting assigned a writing tutor, which will only mean more work. And humiliation.

The Enchantress seems to have put a curse on me. And it follows me through the rest of the week until Friday, when they send progress reports home.

"Josh," Mom says when I emerge from my room and collapse on the couch. "Do you have something for me?"

Everyone in our school district, whether they are in the middle school or high school, gets their progress reports on the same day. And of course Princess Perfect, the model student, went and showed hers off the moment Mom walked through the door.

"Yeah," I say reluctantly. There's no point in lying to Mom. She knows.

A moment passes in silence. I'm not going to make it easy.

"Could I see it, please?" she says. She won't be deterred from torturing me.

I shrug and hand it over. I doubt any training from ninja school covers how to neutralize your mom when she's about to chew you out. Blow darts, nunchucks, and throwing stars just won't cut it against this foe.

Mom takes one look at the report and sits down in the kitchen chair, shaking her head. Three times she almost starts to say something, then stops herself. Lindsay and I stand there, rooted to our spots.

"Josh, I'm sorry I can't be around as much to help you with your homework or to make sure you study. But this can't happen."

"I'll study more," I offer. "Really." And I mean it. Seeing her so stern makes me feel like a tiny person a couple of pixels tall.

She shakes her head. "No, we need to fix this. I'm going to check every night that all your homework is done."

Then she drop-kicks my entire life.

"And no video games or computer until the end of the quarter. You don't need any distractions. Those things are rotting your brain."

"WHAT?" I stare at her, frozen like she's hit me with a stun spell. No video games? At all?

"I'll lock up your consoles," she says. "You'll get them back when you get your report card for this quarter. If the grades have improved."

I shoot her a look of utter horror.

Mom shakes her head. "I'm sorry, Josh, I have to do this. Be glad I'm not telling you that you can't hang out with your friends."

Yeah, as if I have lots of friends at this new school. Or any friends, for that matter. I didn't have time to make any at the last two she pushed me into. And somehow the idea that she assumes I do, and the reality that I don't, makes it ten times worse. Doesn't she realize that none of this would have happened if we hadn't moved? Of course, she thinks it's all my fault.

I stand there silently as Mom goes up the stairs, heading straight to my room. Or at least, the place that we call "my room." It's another in the series of spaces that my stuff's been shoved in. It certainly isn't my home. And without my games, how can it ever really be called "my room"?

A poisonous cloud of red rage swirls around my head. How am I going to survive this?

"If you'd put the effort you put into your games into the rest of your life, you'd do fine," Lindsay says.

I glare at her. What does she know? Princess Perfect, with her great grades, sports team, and cool friends.

"Shut up, Linds!" I yell.

She looks at me for a second, her face screwed-up all funny. "I was trying to help," she says in a strained voice, and storms off.

When Mom comes down with her arms full of my games, I stumble upstairs and collapse onto my bed. I thought I had a great plan with my ninja strategy, but it's backfired in epic fashion. I can feel another life draining out of me. Which, according to the Ancient Unchanging Laws of the Gaming Universe, means I have just one left.

It's much tougher than I imagined it would be to go without games, or even TV. It's not just having nothing to do—it's not having anything to think about, nothing to look forward to. At first I distract myself by rereading a few of my favorite science fiction books, but reality starts to set in by Sunday night. With no computer, I put up a sheet of paper to mark time with a tally on the wall. The end of the quarter is in four weeks. That means four weeks with no electronics.

My wall is covered with all the pictures I've been drawing at school, stuff like Mario sparring with the Prince of Persia, Professor Layton saving Princess Zelda, and Minecraft Guy and Sora from Kingdom Hearts riding a rollercoaster at Disney World.

I pull out a notepad and sit there drawing Luigi punching his way through a brick building that looks a lot like my school, when suddenly I have a brainstorm.

I'm furious with my mom, with my teachers, with my life. Dad always told me, when I got mad at a video game, "Turn your anger into resolve to level up. Make it your need to increase your skills and win." And then, when I would tell him how I was going to do better tomorrow, he'd bring out his favorite saying. In happier times it only applied to little things like cleaning my room or taking out the trash. "If you have something hard to do, the best time to start is now."

A lot of the people in my real life seem almost like characters from a game. Ms. Pritchard is an enchantress; that one is easy. Mr. Ramirez is the owner of a Pokémon Gym, who only speaks in numbers and equations. Mr. Barrington is a dragon who spews out flames with every shout. And of course there's the Mitten Monster, the giant mitten-shaped beast, throwing deadly explosive mittens at anyone who approaches. I sketch them out on several pages of graph paper and pin them to my wall.

I try drawing myself as a silent but deadly ninja, but that doesn't feel right. Hiding and pretending there's nothing wrong has only made everything worse.

At this point I'm starting to hallucinate, stuck there in my prison cell in the high tower of Queen Mom's castle. Have I been doing everything wrong? What sort of game *is* this?

It certainly isn't like a ninja game, where you start out able to sneak, jump from rooftop to rooftop, and fling throwing stars at your enemies. No, it's more like an adventure game. One of the ones where you start out with three hit points, armor made out of old potato sacks, and a balsa-wood sword.

In every adventure game the character starts out at the bottom. A level-one scrub. No skills, powers, or magic items. And if I want to reach the top, to become the hero who could get the grades, beat the bullies, and maybe even impress a princess, there's only one way. I have to grind my way through the levels. I need to learn the rulebook, earn the experience points, max out my stats, and level up.

I've been playing not to lose. It's time to play to win.

# CHAPTER 4

# MAKE LIFE TAKE THE LEMONS BACK

Monday, after school, I get out my biggest sketchpad and make a chart for my wall. It will track all the things I do, from homework to studying to trying to make friends. For each accomplishment I'll mark down experience points. I add in levels, spots for new skills, the whole deal. The goal will have to be to earn experience every day and get a steady chain going, with a mess of boxes filled in every week. I want to be able to look back and see it covered in green ink.

The first stop on any heroic journey is always the same. You need a wise sorcerer to guide your hand. Sometimes you get a prophecy, sometimes you get a totally sweet magic sword, sometimes you get a firm push forward. I don't have Gandalf, Dumbledore, or Obi-Wan Kenobi in my contacts, so I'm going to have to go with my local enchantress: Ms. Pritchard.

The next day I sit through class in her enchanting studio, watching the shadows cast by other kids' heads and the lamps around the room. At the end I gather my books up slowly and wait for everyone to leave. Then I take a deep breath and walk up to her altar of power, strewn with student papers from the past week.

I'm sure, given her mystical powers, that she knows what I'm here for. But she just looks up and says, "Hi, Josh, what can I do for you?"

"I, uh . . ." I've been thinking about this all morning, and still I somehow don't know what to say. She looks back, waiting expectantly. I guess they must teach patience in enchanting school.

"I need to get better grades," I blurt out. Adventurers like me, we're not known for fancy talk.

Ms. Pritchard smiles and nods. "Josh, if you want better grades, make sure to do all your assignments. But is that what you really want?"

". . . Yes?" I venture. This is a trap. I know it's a trap. Wise sorcerers never give you a straight answer.

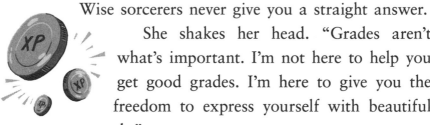

She shakes her head. "Grades aren't what's important. I'm not here to help you get good grades. I'm here to give you the freedom to express yourself with beautiful words."

"Okay," I say, nodding. Do I believe it? No. But sometimes you have to trust that your wise sorceress knows what she's talking about. After all, she's the one with the crystal ball.

I can't tell if Ms. Pritchard is gullible or just going along with it, but she gives me a bunch of advice on how to relax, listen to my muse, and let my brilliance flow out onto the page. It involves tea, meditation, and connecting with your inner Shakespeare.

I resolve to finish all my writing assignments. If you don't do the work, you don't get the experience—and you can't level up.

Her methods seem kooky, but that night I actually give it a try. I have something hard to do. I get Mom's tea down from the high shelf in the pantry and brew a pot. I would do it fancy like in the old British World War II movies Dad used to watch, but I don't know how that works, with the leaves and the little metal thing. So I nuke a mug of hot water and toss in a tea bag and about a quart of honey.

I flop onto the couch with my laptop, which Mom made me promise to use only on schoolwork, and only in the living room. It's like she doesn't trust me not to play video games when no one is looking. She can be a pretty smart lady.

I pop in some headphones and pull up a station of classic rock. Ms. Pritchard said classical music, but it's basically the same thing, right?

I close my eyes for a moment, focusing in on my blissful spot like Ms. Pritchard suggested. Maybe if I tap into some deep reserve of Zen, I'll be able to learn metalbending or something.

Moments later, I can feel the power coursing through me. My eyes shoot open. My hands fly over the keyboard. A tale appears on the page, a short story about a lovesick robot who saves the president from time-traveling mutant assassins.

Not having video games is making me a bit loopy.

The other subject I really need to get on track is math, so the next day I venture into Mr. Ramirez's math Gym. Now, I know there's no chance of ever beating the Gym Leader. Mr. Ramirez is a former math prodigy and I'm just a kid. But if I can at least evolve my skills and have a belt of math Poké Balls, filled with Percentitar, Fractionite, and Geomitrosaur, I'll be all set.

I approach Mr. Ramirez after class. I want to apply the knowledge I've learned from Ms. Prichard, so I start with "I want to learn to express myself better through math."

Mr. Ramirez raises an eyebrow, like he does when a student forgets to reduce a fraction properly. I guess he and Ms. Pritchard have different styles.

"I want to get better grades," I say. "I, uh, want to evolve my Percentitar for this next test." I shake my head. "Sorry, that's weird, what I mean is—"

He laughs. And then he reaches into his coat pocket and lays a handheld on the table. He flicks it on. It's paused on a portrait of Charizard about to use Blaze.

"You like Pokémon?" he asks.

"Yeah, totally!"

Mr. Ramirez smiles. "I don't tell students this normally. It gives them the wrong idea. I was about your age when Pokémon was first released. I have played every game, from *Red* and *Blue*, which were in black and white, to *Black* and *White* . . . which were actually my first color games. I've been playing in the morning on the bus every day since the new one came out last month."

I'm shocked. I'd always thought of our teachers as relics of an ancient era, dinosaurs who somehow wore khakis and ties and stood in front of the classroom lecturing us about the difference between radius and diameter.

"So, Josh, how do you get your Pokémon to evolve?"

"Um . . . battling other Pokémon?"

Mr. Ramirez leans forward in his chair. "Right. But more generally, through practice. You have to battle the math problems. You are a smart guy—but you've got to do your homework. And scribbles before class don't cut it. Each time you skip an assignment, the one after gets harder."

"Yeah, okay," I say. Just doing all my home-  work . . . I was really hoping for some kind of hack or trick. But I guess he has a point. I've never really tried doing a hundred percent of the homework. Thinking about it, it does seem kind of obvious.

"I'm sure you can do it," Mr. Ramirez says. "If you can understand the strategy of Pokémon, you can understand the mysteries of algebra. And if you can get an A in the class this year, I'll let you challenge me in Pokémon."

That thought carries me through the next few days. I've collected hundreds of Pokémon, and my combos are sick. I just need to do the same for math class.

Doing my math homework is a lot less fun than writing stories for English, but I don't have anything better to do, with my video games gone. And there's that chart on the wall, staring at me every day. Sitting around feeling sorry for myself isn't going to fill up my Wall of Heroes. So I resolve to battle the math problems and get ready to take on my Gym Leader. (Okay, realistically, taking on former-child-prodigy Mr. Ramirez isn't very likely. But an adventurer has to dream big.)

Talking to my teachers is actually the easy part. The really intimidating part is on Friday. My first writing tutor session with Maya.

We meet in the cafeteria, which feels weird because it's so empty at the end of the day. The main lights are off and there's no one but Ms. Pritchard, a couple other tutoring sessions, and the staff closing up for the day.

I've been nervous all week. I turned my story in on Wednesday, and the instant I handed it to the Enchantress I wondered if I should have done something a little more traditional. Guys and girls in olden times who won't admit they love each other, old men talking about how hard life is—you know, the sort of thing they make you read in English class. I wrote it in one night, and only really thought about the fact that Maya was going to read it once it was turned in. If I'd paid more attention to that, I might have done something a little less weird.

Maya sits down across from me. I glance down at the paper she set on the table. It's marked up in purple pen, covered with notes and corrections. I instantly feel a lump in the pit of my stomach. She must think I'm a complete weirdo.

"Hi, Josh," she says.

"Hi," I answer, swallowing hard.

She spreads out the papers in front of her. The purple carnage stretches across all of them, and there's a paragraph of writing on the last page. I wish I had Link's power from *A Link Between Worlds*, where he can turn into a painting on the wall and scoot off.

She looks up at me and smiles.

"Okay, Josh," she starts. "First off, your story is a lot of fun!"

"Really?" I ask, a bit shocked. Maybe she's being nice to cushion the blow of having to tell me how messed up it was.

"Yeah, I liked it. I love anything with time travel and lasers. And Commander Toughcookies is such a wild character." She smiles again, and it really feels sincere. Maybe she actually liked it?

"Wow, thanks," I say. I've started to notice that every time she smiles, her nose crinkles up in a way that I find really cute. It's kind of a big contrast to her clothes, which always have an unexpected zipper or swoop to the cut— strange in a kind of cool way. Definitely not "cute." I do my best to ignore both things and focus on the story.

"Don't worry about all these marks," she says, gesturing to the papers. "We'll go over them, but they're just little tweaks. It will only take a few minutes to put them in.

There are a couple big-picture questions I wanted to talk about."

I nod, having to fight not to crane my head over to read her comments early.

"When Commander Toughcookies grabs on to Emotionbot and they travel through the temporal vortex  to the Jurassic era, shouldn't that reverse the entire Invisible Assassins timeline?"

I rock back in my chair and stare at her with my mouth open. Not because she's right (though she totally is) but because she's taken the time to read the story so closely.

We spend fifteen minutes talking about my story, getting into the details and the characters. Then Ms. Pritchard walks over, peering down at us over her glasses.

"How are you feeling about the work, Josh?"

"This is . . . actually kind of fun," I say. "Maya's got some really cool ideas."

"I thought you might get along," Ms. Pritchard says. Enchantresses have pretty good intuition about these things, I guess. "So, Josh, would you characterize your story as person vs. self, person vs. person, person vs. nature, or person vs. society?" She has been teaching us about the different types of narratives for the past week.

"I guess person vs. person. Commander Toughcookies has to defeat all kinds of bad guys."

Maya smiles. "But it's also a bit of person vs. self. Toughcookies does have to face his internal demons in order to save the day."

The Enchantress smiles. "Make sure you focus clearly on one, like a hawk spotting its prey and diving for the kill. Josh, were you able to draw on personal experience?"

I nod. "Yeah, I have to rip apart robots with my bare hands pretty much every day."

We all laugh. For a second I feel like part of some sort of secret society. It's weird to laugh like that with a teacher, as if we all got the same joke. Weird, but kind of cool.

As I'm walking to gym the next Monday, I keep thinking about the types of conflict I have in my life. Person vs. person, with the Mitten Monster haunting my every move. Person vs. environment, trying to survive in a hostile world with no video games. Person vs. society, with a football-obsessed school that doesn't want to accept me. And I guess I have person vs. myself, trying to stay motivated to fill up the Wall of Heroes with successes.

Things would be much easier if all I had to do was beat up a bunch of robots.

When I get to the locker rooms, I double-check which one I'm going into and change as quickly as I can.

We're playing badminton this week, and when we count off, I end up on the team opposite Schmittendorf.

The first time his team serves, Mittens starts in on me.

"Hit it to Creep!" he says.

"No, no, anyone but Creep!" one of his friends, who's on my team, shoots back. I glance at Mr. Barrington. The gym teacher stands there watching as the girl serving hits the shuttle over the net. Luckily, she serves it way out of bounds.

The second time they serve, Mittens makes the same "joke," if you can call it that. And this time the shuttle comes straight for me.

I step up, ready to make him look stupid. Just hit it back, that's all I need to do. Just hit it back and I'll be free.

My racket makes a clanking sound, and the shuttle flies sideways, hitting a girl on my team in the head and falling to the ground.

"Sorry," I mutter, while Mittens and his friends clap sarcastically.

"Good job, Creep. Let's hope beating Lancaster is that easy," one of the other kids says.

I pretend to ignore it, but I'm boiling on the inside. No matter how loud they say it, it's obvious that Mr. Barrington isn't going to do a thing about it. The kids say it like it's just a nickname.

I planned to spend the bus ride home catching up on my math homework, but instead I sit staring out the window while wearing my best Warrior Fury Face. I refuse to let them get to me.

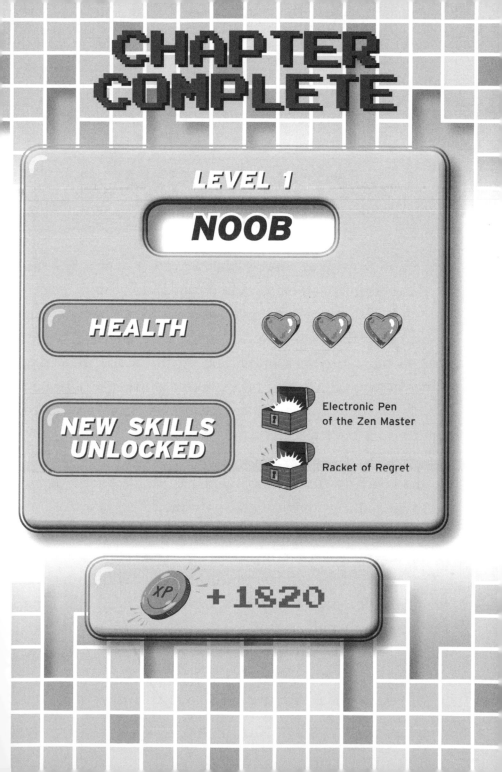

# CHAPTER
# 5

# SUPER SMASHED FACE

Despite some wins at school, when I make it to the weekend I feel drained, like an empty and crushed soda can. I've been without video games for two weeks and it's driving me crazy. Other than schoolwork, I don't have anything to do. I spend the entire weekend sitting on the couch, sketching in my notebook. Mom is taking extra shifts at her second job, so we only see her when she brings home precooked dinner from the supermarket every night.

Finally, on Sunday night, Lindsay stops at my station on the couch, which at this point has molded itself to my butt like a suit of magical elven armor.

"Josh, you didn't *do* anything this weekend," she says. "What's wrong?"

I grunt at her. A well-timed grunt is really a magical thing. People interpret it as "Yeah, I agree with you," but you haven't actually said that. You could really mean anything. Usually it gets my mom or my sister to leave me alone, but this time it doesn't take.

"You sat here drawing for, like, three days straight,"

she says, giving me that you-are-the-most-ridiculous-person-ever-born look.

I shrug. "I can't play video games, it's getting cold outside—what else do I have to do?"

"You need to make some friends. Put yourself out there."

I look up at Princess Perfect. Part of me wants to yell at her. To call her names and make her leave. How is this her business? But she was right about my ninja strategy not working. So I let her keep talking.

"You should do that video game competition thing," she tells me. "Some of the girls in my history class won it when they were in middle school."

"But how, Linds? Everyone already has their teams."

She makes an exaggerated sigh, which only makes me want to throw my notepad at her even more. "And have you actually asked anyone?"

I shrug. Of course I haven't. I sit there, staring at the wall. It's all so easy for her to say, with her instant friends from volleyball and her flawless grades. Princess Perfect doesn't have demonic football players taunting her or impossible math problems stalking her sleep.

"Josh," she says, her brows doing that thing where they get close together when she's about to cry. "Sitting around, doing nothing like this. You're reminding me of two years ago. After—"

"Don't you get it?" I interrupt her. "We never should have left our old town. I'm sure we would have been *fine*.

It's not like Mom has a great job here or anything. And the kids at school call me names."

"So don't let them!" she answers. "Stand up to them!"

"Look," I say. "You don't need to take care of—"

Lindsay cuts me off with an exasperated look, turns, and walks out of the room.

Despite being intensely annoyed at her, I still don't feel like getting up off the couch. Everything seems so hopeless.

But slowly the cloud of rage disappears, like a spell effect wearing off. As the fury evaporates, I realize that Lindsay is right in one way. I need to do something. It doesn't matter that I can't take back the tests I've failed or the mistakes I've made with the kids at school.

 I have to work on what I can control. I don't know how to get friends or make my sister feel better, but I can do what Lindsay said. I can stand up for myself. I might even need to add a new experience point category on the Wall of Heroes.

It doesn't take me long to get my chance. Three days later, I'm standing at my locker holding my sketchbook when I hear a voice behind me that drips with the horror of a thousand dark rituals.

"'Sup, Creep," Mittens says.

"Shut it," I answer. It's the first time I've actually told him to stop.

Not that it works at all, of course!

He stops and spins around to face me, like a shark smelling blood in the water. I can practically see the warning flashing over his head. He's too high level. I don't have a chance against him.

I'm not planning to fight him. I'd get clobbered, obviously. But I can't take it anymore. I have to push back somehow.

He grins at me, a Mitten Monster in full display, puffing himself up to try to look larger. "What ya got in there, Creep?" he asks, pointing at the sketchbook in my hand.

I glare at him. "You, but with a face that's not quite so ugly. No pencil can capture that."

"What?" He stares at me.

A small crowd of kids has stopped in the hallway, watching the face-off.

"Yeah," I continue. My pulse is pounding like I've picked up a speed boost, and in the back of my mind I wonder if I'm writing my death warrant with every word. "And it's too bad that a drawing can't capture your stench."

Mittens laughs sarcastically and turns to walk away. For a moment, I think maybe I've gotten away with it. Then he spins back and swipes the notebook out of my hand. I can hear the page that was open rip as he pulls it away from me, leaving me holding nothing but Snowboard Samurai's head and torso.

"Hey, give that back!" I demand.

"These are awful," he says, leafing through it without really looking. "And sick. Ew, gross. You really are a creep," he taunts. Of course, he's holding the notebook in a way that the other kids can't see any of it.

I've got an active volcano in my chest, ready to erupt.

I can hear the soundtrack of my life ramping up from "dangerous encounter" to "this boss is about to hand your butt to you on a platter" as I step forward. I don't even know what I'm doing anymore. I want him to stop. I can hear that stupid nickname over and over for the rest of my life. Creep. Creep. Creep.

I reach for the notebook, but he pulls it away and pushes me back, slamming me into the lockers, where someone's padlock makes an indentation in my lower back.

Mittens makes a move to push me again and I panic, jumping at him. He must not have expected me to fight back, because we both lose our balance and go down in a tangle, with me somehow ending up on top of him.

He shoves me off like I weigh nothing. In that push I can feel how much stronger than me he is. It's like Young Link wrestling Donkey Kong. I jump back to my feet, but he's faster as well as bigger, and by the time I've stood back up he's swinging his fist at my face.

"Fight!" a boy yells.

I try to duck, but his knuckles connect with my cheek and there's an explosion of galaxies in my vision, mixed with numbers floating in the air showing the massive damage he's done. I stagger, then take a swing back that misses wildly.

"Crush him!" the meaty voice of a jock shouts.

"Yeah, Josh, you go!" a kid yells in mocking singsong.

I step back as Schmittendorf advances, an evil grin on his face. I'm starting to think about running for it when I take another step back and bump up against Stan, one of the linebackers on the football team and one of Mittens's pals. His very large, very muscular pals. I feel like I'm pressed against a wall of meat that smells like sweat and French fries.

"Hey! Hey!" I hear the unmistakable roar of the dragon, Mr. Barrington, far down the hall.

Stan grabs me by the arms, and I'm trapped, with the Mitten Monster winding up to hit me again.

But before he can strike, a voice yells, "Hey, stop it," and a figure comes flying out of the crowd. He isn't big, but he jabs at Stan, who lets go of me to defend himself. I catch a glimpse of the kid when he spins around to face us. It's Peter Andreyev, from my math class. Peter is maybe an inch taller than me and nearly as skinny, and is totally dwarfed by Stan. Peter yells some kind of insult in Russian, and backs off as the linebacker roars.

"Come on!" Peter says, pulling at my shoulder, as the two football players advance on us. We turn to run, and smack right into Mr. Barrington.

"STOP IT!" Mr. Barrington shouts, venting the fury of a dragon who resents having to leave his lair. The kids instantly shut up, but he keeps on yelling at the same volume anyway. "WHAT ARE YOU DOING?"

As soon as Mr. Barrington has taken charge, Mr. Alpert appears, grabbing Stan and the Mitten Monster.

"What happened here?" Mr. Alpert demands, his voice getting even higher than normal in his fury. "Have you boys reverted to being jungle primates? Do I need to put you in a zoo?"

"I'm sure it wasn't Mittens's fault," Mr. Barrington rumbles.

The Frost Giant looks around at the four of us. "You're all facing in-school suspension," he squeaks.

I look around the room, and it's like the scene freezes. I can see exactly where this is going. Mr. Barrington is holding Peter and me, while Mr. Alpert has a much less secure grip on Schmittendorf and Stan. Everything else fades into the blur of the background. I can see the probabilities fluctuating. The four of us have been fighting, none of the teachers saw it start, and so we're all going to end up in detention together. Peter came in to help me, and he's going to take as much blame for it. On the first day of school they'd made a huge deal about their zero-tolerance policy for fighting.

My nose is bleeding all over my favorite shirt (the one where The Doctor is telling Mr. Spock to "Live long and don't blink!") but I stand up straight and look Mr. Alpert in the eye.

"It's my fault," I say. "I started it. Peter and Stan were trying to stop us." It's a lie, but I know that if I try to help only Peter, they won't believe me, and Mittens will contradict me.

Schmittendorf looks at me in shock for half a second, but covers it up. Everyone else, Mr. Alpert included, stares at me in confusion. Finally, Mr. Alpert shrugs. "We'll sort this out. All of you please come to my office. We'll talk this out for as long as it takes."

It's not until I'm in one of the chairs in the cave of the Frost Giant, holding a wad of tissues to my nose, that the adrenaline starts to die down and I stop seeing the world as targets, hit points, and things to dodge. Sitting there while Mr. Alpert arranges papers and pulls out an extra chair, I feel like the condemned hero, waiting for the guards to come and take me to the gallows. And I'm pretty certain that no one will show up at the last minute, shoot through the noose, and lead a blazing getaway. I need a better plan than that. As usual, I wonder what my heroes would do in my situation.

**CHELL FROM PORTAL** would shoot a portal through the window into the parking lot, another one under her feet, and jump through to freedom.

*Strategic Assessment: The Portal gun I got for my eleventh birthday makes lights and noise, but it doesn't seem to actually open apertures between distant points in space-time. I think it's probably defective, but for some reason Mom won't let me send it back.*

**SPIDER-MAN** would use webbing to stick to the ceiling, wait for the principal to come out, and sneak into the office and steal any evidence that linked him to the crime.

*Strategic Assessment: Unfortunately, there are multiple eyewitnesses. Also, the one time I got bitten by a spider . . . no spider powers. I blame Dad for insisting I go to the doctor. How could I mutate once my body was full of antibiotics?*

**SUPERMAN** would stay and face his accusers, bound by honor to obey the law even when he broke it for good reasons.

*Strategic Assessment: Crap. As little as I like it, that's probably the right thing to do. Not to mention that—since I don't have a portal gun or spider powers—I don't have a choice in the matter.*

Eventually, Mr. Alpert comes up with enough chairs and we all sit down. His huge frost giant body seems cramped in the overcrowded cave.

"Boys," he begins, "I know this is a tough time for you. But that isn't an excuse for fighting in the halls!"

He looks directly at me. "Josh, I know that adjusting here has been difficult. But if you have a problem with another student, you should come to me."

Across the room, I can see Schmittendorf grinning at me like he's won the lottery. I've taken the blame for Peter, but in the end, Mittens and Stan have gotten just as much benefit. And if I try to get them in trouble, they'll turn it around on me. I have to sit there and endure their sneering looks every time Mr. Alpert turns his head toward me.

"Why did you start this, Josh? Are there feelings that you need to share with us?"

"I, uh . . ." I'm struggling to come up with a good reason. If I blame Mittens, he'll start fighting back, and then Peter will get in trouble, too. I need a solution that the Frost Giant will accept.

I swallow. "It's been really hard, you know, adjusting to life here. I have a lot of anger." I can see Mr. Alpert nodding. It's totally working. "Henry bumped into me, and I kind of lost it. I'm sorry. Peter and Stan were just trying to pull us apart."

I hate that there's no way to nail Mittens with equal blame, but if there is, I can't think fast enough to come up with it.

The Frost Giant sighs. "I understand that you may have a lot of emotions swirling inside you. But you need to find healthy outlets for them. Violence is never the solution to your problems."

"What about World War Two?" Peter asks, putting on an innocent face.

Mr. Alpert glares at him. "This situation is . . . *rather different*, wouldn't you say?"

"Yeah, okay," Peter doesn't seem convinced, but he drops it.

Mr. Alpert goes on for a while, talking about how school needs to be a safe space for everyone, and that the solution to conflict is to get a teacher, not to start fighting.

I nod along, trying to look like I regret fighting with Mittens. The truth is that the throbbing in my nose is a better reminder of the wisdom of avoiding a fight than the lecture. But the real disaster is the question that has started running through my mind now that the fog of anger has lifted. Where is my notebook?

I check out Mittens and Stan, but unless they've stuffed it up their shirts or something, they don't have it. But his friends were everywhere. Anyone could have picked it up.

And that book has every ridiculous sketch I've done in the past month. Not just the silly ones, but the ones of teachers and students as video game characters. I don't regret the Mitten Monster, but who knows how Ms. Pritchard might feel about her enchantress portrait. And . . . I gulp. And Maya as a punk princess throwing commas like they're ninja stars—which is basically what she did to my story for English class. I'm not so good with the whole "correct punctuation" thing.

Finally, Mr. Alpert gets to the part we've been waiting for, like we've been sitting through a boring love scene in a movie in order to get to the exploding stuff afterward.

"Peter, Stan, and Henry," he says, "I saw that you were all quite clearly fighting. Even if you didn't start it, that can't be tolerated in this school. You'll each have detention after school this week." My stomach sinks. I'd tried to help Peter, but he's still getting it bad. He's going to hate me. "Josh, for starting a fight, you get the same, plus two days in-school suspension."

"Does this mean . . ." Mittens starts, panic wiping the smirk off of his face.

Mr. Alpert nods. "Yes, it means you can't go to practice or the game on Friday. That's school policy."

"But I need to play. Everyone's counting on me!"

Mr. Alpert shrugs. "The policy is meant to be a punishment, Henry. I'm sorry. The rules say that you can't participate in extracurriculars while you're serving detention."

The crushed look on Mittens's face as we stand up to leave makes me feel like I just pulled out a Smash Bros. sudden death tiebreaker. Mr. Alpert takes us to get our things from our lockers before going out to meet our parents. While we were in his office everyone had gone home, and the school is silent. Every little sound echoes down the halls.

I check the area around my locker for the notebook. Nothing but a few scraps that ripped when Mittens and I fought over it. Someone picked it up. For all I know, they spent the last period of the day showing it to everyone and laughing at me.

Schmittendorf's dad arrives first, picking up him and

Stan. While Mr. Alpert goes down to talk with the three of them, I turn to Peter.

"Thanks for helping me out, but I'm sorry you got caught in this. I tried to get you out of it, but—"

He cuts me off, with a huge grin on his face. "Are you kidding? That was EPIC. And besides, I couldn't let those jerks gang up on you."

I stare back at him, realizing that the only person at Howard Taft Middle School who would stick up for me is probably a maniac with a death wish. My first impression was right: definitely a rogue.

"When I first moved here from Moscow, I barely spoke any English," he says. "When they didn't ignore me, they called me names. And at recess they would speak in fake Russian, hold me down, and spit in my hair."

"Wow," I say. I guess he has kind of a decent reason for holding a grudge.

"Oh, there's my mom. Catch ya later, guy!" he says, punching me lightly on the arm and running for his mom's van.

Mr. Alpert is still talking to Mittens's dad, who looks like a six-foot-five version of Mittens, but with a big fat gut instead of muscles. He's red in the face and his voice is like a foghorn. Mittens stares at the ground while his dad yells, but when he looks up and sees me watching, he scowls.

"You've got to be kidding me!" Mr. Schmittendorf shouts. "The team needs Henry—he's the only one on the team who can catch anything. They'll never beat Lancaster without him!" He glares at his son. "And don't get me started with you, kid. That's the one you were fighting with? You telling me you couldn't keep a scrawny kid like that from knocking you over? What are you gonna do when the Lancaster defense comes at you? They're twice his size!"

Mr. Alpert tries to say something, but Mr. Schmittendorf ignores him and keeps yelling while the boys get in the car. Finally they drive away.

I know my mom had to leave work to come get me, so I don't blame her for being late. When she does come, she steps out of the car before I can get in.

"Again, I'm so sorry, Mr. Alpert," she says. They must have already had a conversation when he called to tell her I had missed the bus and needed to be picked up. I'm just glad I've been spared the humiliation of having to call or text her myself.

I'm expecting her to scream at me, but we spend the ride home in icy silence. It's almost worse than being yelled at. Her lips are pursed, and she has a white-knuckle grip on the steering wheel, like when I hold the controller in the final lap of a Mario Kart cup race. She doesn't look over at me once, the whole time.

After a ride that seems to last three times longer than normal, we pull into the driveway. I try to head straight for my room, but when we get to the living room Mom grabs my shoulder in a kung fu death grip and guides me to the couch.

"Josh, you know I love you," she says.

I gulp and nod. This is not a good sign.

"But getting in a fight at school? Really?" she says. It's almost a relief, an end to the silence. "And Mr. Alpert said that you *started* it. I know you can't control everything that happens at school, but you can't be starting fights."

I nod again, not knowing how to respond to the rising volume of her voice.

"We're having a hard enough time as it is, without you getting in trouble. I had to take off from the bank early to come pick you up. The bank manager gave me such a look when I told him . . . and what would happen if you had actually gotten suspended instead of in-school suspension? I can't take any more days off work. I can't."

On the other hand, she's the one who decided to move here, someplace where I don't fit in even a little bit. But I can't say that.

"And you don't even seem to try at school," Mom went on, her volume rising steadily. "Your sister is already testing into the advanced track, and you're barely passing your classes. It's like you don't care."

Of course I don't care about school. How can I, when every time I get settled, we pack up and move somewhere else?

"Josh, can you tell me what the heck you were thinking? What possibly possessed you to do this?" she demands, not actually giving me the time to answer her questions. "What would your dad think of—"

And then she runs out of energy, like someone pulled the power plug.

If Dad were still around, I wouldn't be getting into fights. We wouldn't have had to move, and I would still have friends. But I can't tell Mom that. "Mom, I got in a fight. I'm okay, it's fine."

She sighs. "And this was supposed to be one of the suburbs with the good schools."

My old school was a good school. One where I had friends, and hadn't missed big chunks of math class.

Back when Dad was alive and Mom was still around enough to pay attention to me and not just yell at me and take my stuff away.

# CHAPTER
# 6

# IT'S DANGEROUS TO GO ALONE

The next morning I stumble out of bed and get ready in a stupor, moving automatically. I brush my teeth and shower. In the mirror, I can see the thousand-yard zombie stare in my eyes. No feelings or thoughts. Just routine. Mom has already gone to work, but there's breakfast on the table and a note saying *I love you guys. Have a great day!*

Maybe she has somehow repressed the fact that I'm going to spend the day suffering through in-school suspension. Or maybe she thinks I deserve it and doesn't care.

On the bus I slide down as low as I can and try to draw in a fresh notebook. But everything comes out jagged, messy, and ugly. Writing a page for homework on the bus is hard enough, but drawing is impossible.

From the moment I walk through the front doors of the school, I know something is off. A girl glares at me over her books, with rage in her eyes that could almost power a deadly curse.

I look ahead and walk down the hall. To my left, I can

hear a boy's voice in a fake whisper. "He's the one. It's all his fault."

"He probably did it on purpose," a girl answers.

I keep walking.

"Wait, what did he do?" a kid says.

"He got Mittens detention," another adds, her voice hissing with fury.

I keep walking, no matter what I hear in the whispers weaving their way through the school around me.

Being in detention may almost be a relief—I won't have to face all of these kids. A minute later I'm standing in front of my locker, staring into the depths of Vault 151 and contemplating my fate. If someone looks at those drawings, it will be disastrous. I've drawn video game versions of half the kids in my classes. And Mittens is featured prominently. If he finds out that I've still been drawing parodies of him . . .

Trying to think back through what was in that sketchbook, I realize that the last few pages had a bunch of doodles of Maya, the Punk Princess. I can feel my face flushing in embarrassment already, knowing what people will think if they see those. What *she* will think.

I gaze into the shadowy depths of Vault 151. Wishing some sort of answer would tumble out of it.

"Hey, Josh, are you okay?"

I turn. It's Maya, with her face all knit up in worry. I can tell she's staring at the bruise on my face.

I shrug. "Yeah, I'm fine. I have in-school suspension. Sorry I'm going to miss our next meeting. I've been working on the writing."

She shakes her head. "That doesn't matter—I'm just glad you're okay. I arrived when that linebacker had you pinned."

I shudder. For a second I feel again the helplessness of that huge guy holding me while the Mitten Monster swings to put a dent in my skull. "Yeah, I lucked out. This could have been a lot worse, I guess," I say, pointing to my nose.

"Don't get in any more fights, okay?" she says, as she pulls off her backpack and opens it up. I can't quite tell whether she's concerned or annoyed.

"You don't need to tell me that. I almost got crushed. Anyway, I have to head to detention. Probably not a good idea to be late for that."

"Sure," she says. "But this is yours, isn't it?" She reaches into her backpack, roots around for a minute, and pulls out a sketchbook.

I stare down with what I'm sure is a really dumb jaw-hanging-open look.

"I found it on the floor when the teachers made everyone clear out after the fight. You had it during our meeting last week, right? The Pikachu on the back cover is really cool."

"Yeah, definitely. Thanks so much. This is amazing!" I say breathlessly. "I . . . I have to run," I say, grabbing the notebook. "Thanks again."

Worrying about the sketchbook took a bunch of time, and I'm actually five minutes late for detention, which earns me another lecture from Mr. Alpert. But I don't care. I got my notebook back. There will be no humiliation in front of the whole school. For the first hour, I sit there trying not to look happy. Mr. Alpert has ended up with the privilege of sitting in the empty classroom with me. He looks over occasionally and shakes his head, as if disappointed and shocked that I'm making him waste his time like this.

But as time drags on, intense boredom sets in. And I can't stop wondering whether Maya looked in my notebook, and if she saw the pictures of herself. She would have mentioned it, wouldn't she? She did say something about the cover. I can only hope that she just glanced at it and didn't actually look through the pictures. Knowing that it's not getting passed around at lunch today makes me feel like I dodged a huge lava pit.

By the end of the first day of in-school suspension—which is basically just sitting in an empty classroom with nothing to do—getting in a fight finally starts to feel like a huge mistake. I do my homework within the first few hours, and even get a few days ahead. I thought that not having to listen to teachers drone on would be kind of nice, but by the late afternoon I'm longing to hear the Enchantress talk about putting ourselves into personal essays, the math Gym Leader tell us how to cancel fractions, or even the Dragon roaring about the importance of proper gym clothes.

And when I go to the bathroom every couple hours, I have to look in the mirror and stare at the big black-and-blue bruise in the middle of my face.

Sitting in detention, I have an endless expanse of time to think about it. In the end, getting my sketchbook back, having Peter there to help me, not get-ting my nose completely broken—I really lucked out. It's only dumb luck that getting in a fight didn't end in game over. And it hasn't solved anything. Schmittendorf only hates me more now.

I spend the next day in the same lockdown, watching Mr. Alpert read a book called *Connecting With the Tween Mind*. It would be cool, though a bit creepy, if he was learning telepathy, but it's probably more junk about emotions. I just hope he doesn't decide to practice on me.

We have to change rooms periodically to find a new empty one. Walking from one to the other with the Frost Giant looming over me, I can feel the stares of the kids even more strongly. It's like they installed lasers in their eyes while I was in detention.

The weekend arriving should be a relief, but when the bell rings and I get up to walk out, Mr. Alpert hands me a thick folder.

He looks down at me from the thin air up where his head is. "I know that was difficult," he says slowly, "but I hope you recognize the necessity of punishments to keep our school safe."

"Oh, yeah, definitely," I answer. "I don't want to go through that again." And I mean it. The thought of another fight makes my nose throb like it's going to explode. My hit points are dangerously low.

On Monday I think the torment will be over, but my life only doubles down on awful. I can see the looks even before I get into the lobby.

"He was sitting on the bench because of you," some girl says. I look back at her dumbly.

A boy spits at me. Well, not at me. In my general direction, from about twenty feet away. But I still shrink inside. What have I done?

"What are you, on Lancaster's side?" someone else says.

"Yeah, where did you say you moved from, anyway?" comes an angry voice from behind me.

"We only needed one touchdown! And Kevin dropped it!" another guy chimes in. "YOU TOOK AWAY OUR MITTENS!"

I rush to class, not bothering to stop at my locker and drop my books. It's one of those levels where there are spikes, lava, cannonballs, and enemies all at the same time.

As I sit waiting for Ms. Pritchard to start her class, I hear more of them from behind me.

"It's *his* fault," a girl's voice hisses. "That Buster kid. Schmittendorf wasn't there because they got in a fight."

"Yeah," some boy says. "And I heard the new kid started it."

I carefully stare forward, pretending not to listen.

"Mittens would have caught that pass," the girl says. "He always comes up with it."

"Yeah," the boy agrees. "And that new kid—Jeffery? Jeremy? Without him attacking Mittens, we would have beaten Lancaster."

"Biggest game of the year, and this Jeff kid blows it for us."

Finally understanding makes my head hurt even more, like one of those traps where the walls close in until they crush you. And these kids who hate me don't even know my name. Last week there were announcements about a pep rally for the game, and I remember seeing a bunch of boys wearing jerseys on Friday when I walked in to suspension. I forgot about it when I was locked away in the Frost Giant's Cave of Deprivation.

No one at my old schools paid much attention to sports. Here they care about football the way I care about a new Zelda game coming out. I've seen them in between classes, watching online videos of the players from the high school team and speculating which ones will get recruited by the big colleges.

Because of the fight, Schmittendorf was in detention and didn't play in the game on Friday. And it sounds like our team lost to Lancaster by four points. Which, in the twisted and illogical imaginations of the fans, makes me responsible for our team losing.

Through the day it doesn't get any better. I can tell

from every passing look that kids are judging me. I try to rush through the halls as fast as I can, avoiding eye contact and slumping my shoulders to stay small. But I can still hear the comments.

In kindergarten they tell you that standing up to a bully will somehow make him leave you alone. Maybe that works when you're six years old. But even after we both got in trouble, Schmittendorf keeps at it.

When I get to gym, I walk into the locker room as he is walking out. My whole body tenses for impact, but he just says, "Creep," and nods at me, a scowl plastered on his face.

He doesn't need to do anything, and knows it. The other kids are doing his work for him.

That day in gym it's "Creep" this and "Creep" that, and not just from Mittens. Everyone gets in on the action, to the point that even Mr. Barrington tells Stan to cut it out.

"Stan, give him a break," Mr. Barrington says when the big linebacker is harassing me, while we're sitting on the bleachers waiting for our turn. "It was our defense that lost on Friday. Having Mittens wouldn't have kept Lancaster from scoring three times."

Stan glares at me, his lip curling up. I look away, trying to stay calm while my heart flutters like a tin can tied behind a car.

"Leave him alone," Maya says from the court. "The receiver dropped that pass, not Josh."

Stan grunts in return, but at least he stops talking for a few minutes.

I'm grateful to Maya for saying something, but it almost makes it worse. Now she sees me as some poor kid who needs her help. Not just in writing, but in life, too.

I'm sure that makes me an attractive guy. There's nothing like pity to make a girl think you're cool.

When I get home from school that day, I collapse on the couch and don't move until Mom gets home hours later and leaves Chinese takeout on the dining room table before heading out to the cell phone store.

I'm completely drained of energy, but I can't even get upset about it. Why should I get to be happy, anyway? I should be used to this by now.

I'm sitting in Mr. Ramirez's room before class the next day when Peter slides into the desk next to me.

"Whoa, sweet shirt, man," he says.

"Uh, thanks," I answer. I look down at my chest. It's my favorite T-shirt, the one with Sonic the Hedgehog running past Mario and Bowser in their Mario Kart go-karts. I love this shirt, but the last couple weeks I haven't really been paying much attention to what I wear. I just put on whatever's at the top of the drawer. "Thanks again for helping me," I add. "If you hadn't jumped in, my face would have been flattened into 2-D."

"Hah, no worries," Peter says. "Can you believe Mittens missed his big game? It's just so sweet."

"Yeah, I guess." I'm not so sure it's a good thing for me, but I figure I might as well let the guy be happy.

 "Listen," Peter says, leaning over. "Chen, Taniko, and I are going to play Smash Bros. at my house after school and need a fourth, want to come?"

I feel jittery, like that time I "accidentally" downed one of Mom's triple espressos and couldn't sleep for thirty hours.

"Sure, yeah," I answer. "That would be great."

"You realize that we're, like, ridiculously awesome at it, right?" Peter raises an eyebrow. "I hope you're more into it than just having that T-shirt you wore the other day."

I look him in the eye and nod.

He sighs with relief. "Good, because I already told Taniko and Chen that we're going to make them wish they'd never picked up a controller."

Before I can reply, Mr. Ramirez asks us to quiet down so that he can start class. I'm a little distracted thinking about which character I'll pick to be the most impressive in our first game. Should I go for Luigi and play my best, or save it to show off later? Luckily I actually did my homework while I was suspended, so I'm not completely lost. This was one of the units we did in math last spring, at least. It seems like half the time I'm ahead and half the time I'm behind.

Between classes I send Mom a text saying I'm going to a friend's house after school. *Joshie, I'm so glad, have a great time!* she writes back. I've asked her, like, a hundred times not to call me Joshie, but she still does it any time she's happy with me.

Since in theory I'm banned from playing video games and in trouble at school, I let it slide this time.

We all meet up by the flagpole to head to Peter's house. When I get there, Chen is showing Taniko and Peter something on his phone.

"They're going to *destroy* me," he's saying. "My dad made me promise three times to be careful. My mom even offered to knit a protective case for it."

Peter laughs. "I'm sure it would have looked super hip. You should have her do it."

"Would it have cute little reindeer dancing with Santa, like the sweater she made you wear to the school Christmas party?" Taniko asks.

I glance at the phone over Taniko's shoulder. There's a small jagged crack at the very top of the screen.

"What happened to it?" I ask.

Chen shrugs, scowling. "I left it in my pocket during gym. Which was stupid. It flew out of my pocket and hit the bleachers."

"The crack kind of looks like a little lightning bolt," I say. "And it survived something that should have killed it. I guess it's the Phone Who Lived."

Everyone laughs, and Chen seems to relax a bit. I'm a little embarrassed at how good it feels to make a dumb joke like that and have someone get it. These are my people.

"Don't tell them," Peter suggests.

Chen shakes his head. "I'm not good at hiding things. My mom will know something's up immediately."

"Sorry, man," Peter says. "Looks like you're getting a sweet, sweet knitted phone case, then. I promise to only talk trash about it while my mouth is open."

Peter's basement turns out to be huge, with carpeting not just on the floor but on the walls as well. He has big recliners, a massive TV, and two full generations of game consoles—not to mention a fridge, Foosball, Ping-Pong, and air hockey. When I die and pass on to Valhalla, forget endless feasting and brawling—I want the Carpeted Dungeon.

I'm looking around in awe when Chen sidles over to me.

"Awesome, right?" he says in a whisper even softer than his usual voice. "I'm pretty sure Peter's parents are in the Russian Mafia."

"Ugh," Peter says from the other side of the room. "How many times do I have to tell you, Chen? They're both dentists. They met at dental school. They're the least criminal people you'll ever meet."

Chen shrugs, as if Peter's story can't change his conclusion.

"Josh, think fast," Peter says as I'm walking over to check out the Foosball table.

I look up, and it must have looked like I was hit with a freeze spell as a soda can whizzes by my ear, ricochets off the couch cushions, and comes rolling back to rest at my feet.

"Oh, uh, hey, I'm really sorry," I stammer.

Peter glances down at the can sitting at my feet. "No spill, no foul."

"The dents add flavor," Taniko adds.

We all laugh, and I feel a wave of relief.

"Okay, let's do this," Peter says when we're all settled in. "Dibs on Sonic!"

"Yeah, 'cause you want to be able to run away like always," Taniko says. "I'm Dr. Mario, and your prescription today is defeat and sorrow."

"Bowser will sit on you and crush you until you're only two dimensional," Chen says.

"I'll, uh, play Luigi," I say. Did I need a clever quip? "And . . . I'll think up some great trash talk for next time."

"They can trash-talk all they want," Peter says as the match counts down to start. "But we'll be taking out the trash tonight."

And it's game on.

Peter is laughably bad, but I more than hold my own. In the end we lose a match that was close, only because Peter keeps taking ridiculous risks and getting himself walloped into the abyss.

"Well, Maya's the real Smash Bros. expert," Chen explains after the match is over. "You'll have to play with her."

"Ugh, yeah," Peter says. "But I'm kinda glad she's not here. It's like in the video game design project, she just wants to work all the time. Today she would probably have us running laps in Smash Bros. instead of actually playing."

"If you can call what you just did playing," Taniko says with a snicker.

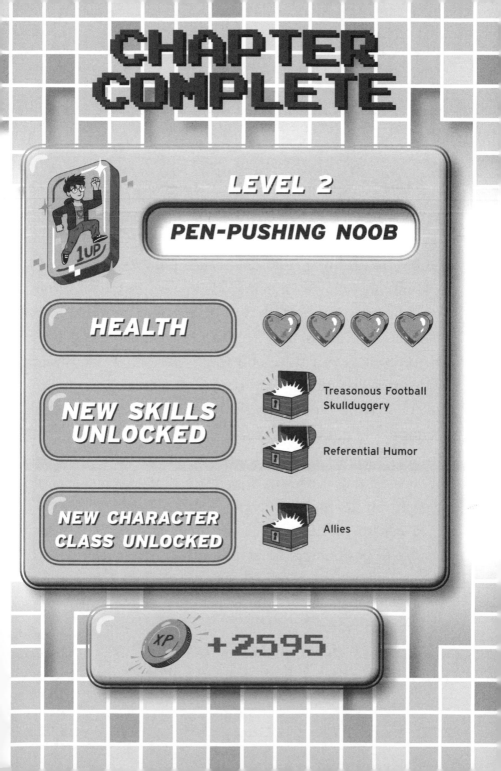

# FIVE O'CLOCK SHADOW OF THE COLOSSUS

I've been awarding myself experience points every night for finishing my homework and studying for tests, and I know I've done a lot better. The Wall of Heroes is starting to get filled in, with thousands of experience points in the bank. The problem is that there's no way to hit "reset" on seventh grade, and first-quarter report card day is here.

They hand them out right before the end of school, so it's not until I'm sitting on the bus that I actually get to look at mine. The whole walk from the lobby to the bus I feel the closing music revving up, but I don't know what it's going to be. Joyful trumpets or sad trombone?

I run to the first seat I can find, not worrying about the usual positioning to stay away from the elementary school goblins with their squeaky voices and snotty noses. Alone, a first grader is cute. In packs, they are a menace to the civilized world.

I scrunch down, my whole body tense as I press my knees into the seat in front of me. I pull the report card out and scan down the columns that will determine my fate for the next quarter.

And the amazing thing is, I survived. Various flavors of Bs, a C+ in math, and I've even gotten an A– in English. Ms. Pritchard must have really liked my reading report on how *Tuck Everlasting* was pro-death propaganda and should be banned for supporting the Grim Reaper's murderous agenda. How can anyone not think that living forever would be totally awesome?

I'm pretty impressed with myself, given that I started the year out suffering under some sort of laziness jinx.

I practically run downstairs when Mom gets in that night.

"Why are you thudding down the stairs, Joshie?" Mom asks.

I shove the report card in her face.

"I did it!"

She grins and examines the report.

"I guess you did," she admits. "Well done. You passed, anyway!"

She leans in and gives me a hug. Which is normally annoying, because lately she squeezes a little tighter than is really necessary, but I don't even mind, because I know what's coming next.

I look at her and raise an eyebrow. "So, this means that . . ."

She nods slowly. "Are you sure you want them back? Maybe you discovered that you don't like them anymore?"

I give her my best witch doctor hex stare.

"But wouldn't you rather spend your time studying and doing math than playing video games? I mean, does anyone even play them anymore?" Apparently she has been building up an immunity to my hexing powers. Moms are sly like that.

She can see the fury in my face, and she cracks up before it goes any further. Then we both start laughing, though mine is a bit more nervous than hers. I won't feel at ease until I actually have a controller in my hand.

I get over the joke pretty quickly, but she's still giggling at her own cleverness as she unpacks my video game systems and brings them down for me. When she puts the cardboard box of games and systems back in my room it feels like my birthday, Christmas, and the last day of school all wrapped into one.

They're a little dusty from the closet, and I clean everything off like it's an archaeological dig. For a minute I sit there staring at the pile of games, not knowing what to do first. They are all there, my old friends with their bright covers, so many memories trapped on each disc. Sure, you can download all of them now, but I still like to have the physical copy if I can get it. Something about the shelf of games makes it feel more like my collection.

There are the Nintendo games, with characters who've been with me since I was a little kid. There are the Final Fantasy games, with their crazy hair and huge swords. I never tell anyone, but I cried a few times in those. Then there are the ones with guns that I keep in the back and don't play when my mom is around. And so many others—swords and sorcery, crazy animals, robots with lasers.

And then, underneath the pile, the sports games that I haven't touched in almost two years. The ones I used to play with Dad after he got home from work, hoping we could get in one more game before Mom called us in for dinner. He would plop on the couch, unbutton his dress shirt to reveal a grimy white T-shirt, and grab the second controller. His face would be covered with stubble and he smelled like sweat after a long day at the bank, but somehow that smell came to feel safe and normal.

It seemed that, with his hands on a controller, Dad would talk freely, way more than he normally would. He'd tell me about the crazy rich people he had to talk out of harebrained investment schemes, and the less-inappropriate half of the dirty jokes his officemate Harry told.

His deal with Mom was that she cooked and he did the dishes, but I can't tell you how many times we would bet his five dollars against me doing the dishes on a game of basketball. And somehow, in those games, he always played way better than usual. You'd be shocked at how many years it took me to figure that trick out.

And when I tried to procrastinate and get him to play one more game, he would shrug and say, "If you have something hard to do, the best time to start is now." He seemed to think his saying was so wise. And since I was doing his chores while he was beating *my* high scores on *my* video game system—well, I guess I have to admit he must have had a certain sort of wisdom.

"Josh, come down for dinner," Mom calls from downstairs. "I made bacon-stuffed cheeseburgers to celebrate your grades."

I look up at the clock and realize I've been sitting here staring at the cover of that basketball game for almost half an hour. It was a couple years out of date even then, but we liked this version. And I swear Dad knew some cheat codes on this one.

I get up, wipe my eyes with the backs of my hands, and go down to the dining room to celebrate.

The next morning on the way to the bus stop, I walk with a new swagger. I've leveled up. Who would have thought that working at something actually made you more successful at it? That doing schoolwork led to parents and teachers not going crazy? I swear that I had no idea that's how it works.

I resolve to keep doing my schoolwork, even though I have my games back. Well . . . most of it, anyway. I'm not making any guarantees. But I promised Mom at dinner last night that I would, and now she knows that taking away

my video games means I get better grades. Which is an
unholy power that no mother should have.

I stare out the bus window as the big-box stores and
apartment complexes roll by. The problem with leveling up
is that once you start, you don't want to stop. My life is
better, but still feels empty. I have my games back, but at
my old school I had friends to play them with.

Which is strange, because I can't remember how I got
those friends in the first place. I guess when you're a kin-
dergartener, making friends over blocks, seesaws, and toy
trucks is a lot easier. Once you grow up and go to middle
school, it's a lot more complicated. What's the trick?

It was fun hanging out at Peter's house, but that was
just the once, and none of them really talked to me much
this past week.

So I call up my usual cast of advisors to try to figure
this one out. How would they make friends?

**YOSHI** would offer to give people a ride on his back
and lick their enemies to death.

   *Strategic Assessment: This seems like a pretty solid
   plan, but I have a skinny back, and I can't even use
   my tongue to whistle properly, so I doubt I can use it
   to defeat bad guys. Not a great outlook on this one.*

**SOLID SNAKE** would speak in a gravelly voice,
make threats, and avoid talking about his feelings at
all costs.

*Strategic Assessment: Solid Snake doesn't actually have any friends. He's cool and all, but as a role model for making friends . . . probably not that useful.*

**MARIO** would jump through world after world, sacrificing everything to try to save Princess Peach. And she would keep getting captured. It seems like every couple years it happens again. It's almost like she's actually in league with Bowser and *wants* to be captured.

>*Strategic Assessment: This whole scenario is starting to creep me out. Mario should probably quit chasing Princess Peach and go do some online speed dating or something. He's got a much better shot at success that way.*

**LINK** would find out what each person in the town wants and then go on epic quests to get it for them.

>*Strategic Assessment: Doing nice things for people. Actually not a bad idea!*

## CLOUD STRIFE FROM FINAL FANTASY

would seek out other noble warriors who share his goals and form up an adventuring party.

>*Strategic Assessment: This is pretty brilliant. You see, Mom? Video games do have important lessons they can teach us. They're not only rotting my brain, they're also teaching valuable social skills.*

I need to find common cause with a group of like-minded adventurers. I step off the bus, narrowly dodging a third grader who seems to think his pencil is a lightsaber. Kind of funny, but I pretend not to notice.

It all comes together as I walk up the stairs to my locker and see one of the signs:

VIDEO GAME DECATHLON

SIGN UP THIS WEEK!

ALL PROCEEDS GO TO THE SPRING FIELD TRIP.

That's it. I know a bunch of kids who are video game nuts like me. Maybe they'll ask me to play with them! Once you've been in an adventuring party with someone, I figure it's going to be much more likely you'll end up friends with them. So I have to hope that they'll ask me to join their party. I remember overhearing Maya and Taniko talking about it earlier in the year.

At the beginning of the day I'm so excited I can barely pay attention in class. I chat with Peter in math, help Chen decipher the corrections in a social studies essay, and have my tutoring session with Maya, but none of them mention it. I hear several other people talking about the Decathlon in the hallway, but I end the day no closer to having an adventuring party. By the time I get home, the nervous energy from the morning is gone. I trudge into my room and toss down my backpack. I do my homework first—

which I almost never do—because video games remind me of my failure today. I go downstairs and sit on the couch for a while after I'm finished, not having the energy to do anything, but not tired enough to sleep. I turn the TV on, and end up watching pro wrestlers taunt one another but never get around to having a wrestling match. Those guys seem to talk about their feelings a *lot*. Solid Snake wouldn't approve.

From the couch, I watch Lindsay come in, disappear into her room to change outfits, and then head back out.

"Hey," she says each time, not even looking up from the messages flying back and forth on her phone. As I lie there, I look down at my phone. Nothing but notifications from annoying games that I don't play anymore. No, I don't want free dragon bucks or a bonus laser cannon for my battle station. Mom isn't going to be home until late tonight, so it's my rumbling stomach that finally gets me off the couch. I make a peanut butter sandwich, grab some milk, and trudge up to my room.

I sit on my bed eating, trying to figure out what could raise my spirits. When I'm done eating I wipe my hands on my jeans and look through my collection, carefully staying away from the ones in the back. But I do look at some of the classics, the games I've kept because I heard they're timeless, like the original *Legend of Zelda* and *Super Mario Bros.* My hand stops on *Final Fantasy VII*.

If I'm trying to form a party, this is one of the best games to show the way. I look at Cloud, standing on the cover with his improbably enormous sword. What would he do?

I sigh. He wouldn't be some loser, waiting around to get asked to join in the fun. He'd go right after whatever he wanted.

That night I lie awake in bed, mind spinning in circles. What if they don't want me? What if they've already made their team? If they wanted me, wouldn't they have already asked me? It all seems so futile.

I finally fall asleep, early in the morning, still flopping back and forth trying to get comfortable. And I swear, in my feverish state, that Sir Lancelot appears to me in a vision.

"Josh Baxter," he says, his voice booming through the halls of Camelot. "You must seek out your companions, for the path of the hero is the path of action."

"But, Lancelot," I complain. "What if they don't want me? What if they've already got a full team?"

The greatest knight of the round table shakes his head and chuckles. "You have to undertake this challenge not because you are guaranteed victory, but to prove that you can make the attempt, to prove yourself worthy. A true hero doesn't wait for the permission of others to undertake his quest."

"But . . ."

"It does not need to make perfect sense, Josh Baxter. It's just a dream," Lancelot intones, and then turns around and demands another flagon of mead, and I wake up to my buzzing alarm.

Now, I can't explain why a hero like Sir Lancelot bothered to take the time to visit a middle school kid and help  him overcome his anxiety, but I appreciate it. And I know he's right. A player character needs to take the initiative. If I want to make this happen, I have to be the catalyst.

So that day in math class, I put the question to Peter, even though I would rather face all the knights of the round table than ask one of my classmates to let me join his video game team.

"Hey, Peter," I say when he sits down across from me.

"'Sup, Bax?" he answers.

"Are you guys doing the Video Game Decathlon? I'm kind of . . . looking for a team." It comes out so lamely, but for a second it feels good to have it out there in the world instead of rattling around inside my head.

Peter shrugs and grumbles, and I feel like an idiot for asking.

He sits there for a minute, looking sour. Finally he turns to me and shrugs.

"Don't feel bad, man. We were going to ask you, since teams can be up to six," he says. Which is a nice thought, but my stomach drops out from the hopelessness in his voice. "But Mittens and his student council friends got ahold of it," he continues. "They changed the format. It's got a bunch of sports games now. We don't play that junk."

As Peter is talking, Chen drops his backpack and slides into the seat behind him.

"You guys talking Decathlon?" He almost growls after he says it. "I can't believe they changed it so much. It's barely even the same thing anymore."

"Last year Chen and I got knocked out in the semifinals when it came down to us versus Maya and Taniko," Peter explains. "When we heard they were changing the game list, we decided to join forces to stay competitive. Also, I'm trying to get Chen to talk to Taniko more, 'cause he has a *ginormous* crush."

"Shut up," Chen says. "You know that it can never happen."

"Dude . . ." Peter starts to argue, then shrugs and gives up, as if he knows how this conversation will go from previous attempts. "Anyway, when the student council released the final list, it had changed too much. There's a bunch of sports games on there now. NBA 2K-something, Football something, NCAA whatever . . ."

"NCAA Soccer. I don't think anyone even watches that on TV, let alone plays the game. I don't know how to play that stuff," Chen says, making a face like he's about to puke. "I don't think they're even real games. The student council said they 'wanted to be more inclusive.' Which means they want it to be more inclusive of us losing."

Peter shakes his head. "So we all got together last week and decided not to do it. Let the jocks win without us competing. That way it won't mean anything."

I've gotten so excited I have to grip the edge of my desk to keep steady.

"I've been playing those games since I was a little kid. My dad and I used to . . . we would always . . ." I struggle to get it out. "Anyway, I've been playing those games for years. I can play them, and I can show you guys how to play for the team ones."

Peter gives me a long look and raises an eyebrow. "Really? How good are you?"

I wonder how skilled I really am. But  would Lancelot back down? No, I don't think so. "Good enough," I say with confidence that I don't feel. "I'll show you."

Peter shrugs. "Okay, let's talk it over with the girls at lunch."

Chen's lip curls up. "I want to *destroy* them."

We both look at him.

"The jocks, not the girls!"

Unfortunately, I don't start off lunch that day with a persuasive argument uniting us all behind one common goal. It doesn't quite go like that.

"Captain America is a meathead with a dinner plate, and Thor is a Labrador retriever with a comically large hammer. Iron Man is a billionaire industrialist!" Peter is saying when I walk up and put my tray down.

"Hulk is a brilliant research doctor, at least when he's not big and green," Chen says, clearly repeating himself. "Why don't you even mention him?"

"Iron Man is a scientist, too," Peter answers. "And he makes things people actually want to use!"

"Uh, what's up, guys?" I mutter as I sit down.

"Smartest Avenger," Maya explains. "It's obviously Black Widow, but they're not listening to me."

"Loki," Taniko says.

"Doesn't count!" Chen protests. "He's a villain!"

"Loki," Taniko insists. "He 'avenges' with the rest of them when it suits his goals."

"What exactly are they supposed to be avenging?" I say, hoping to derail the conversation. "They should be called the Mostly Bad at Teamwork World-Saving Group."

It doesn't work. They dive in further, pulling out a variety of obscure backstory trivia that I've never heard of.

"Do you know that Iron Man and Hulk *both* have multiple PhDs?" Taniko says at one point. "The five most famous Avengers actually have an average of 1.2 PhDs each."

I want to smack my head over and over with my math textbook. Where do my friends find the time?

I hope the Video Game Decathlon will come up naturally at some point, but as lunchtime runs out, I realize that it's not going to be so easy.

In games, you show up and the boss battles happen. You walk in, dodge the cannonballs, shoot some arrows, and you win. In real life, if you want those experience points, it's a little more complicated. Cannonballs and spike pits are more straightforward than conversations. Sometimes it's easier to be Hercules and reroute a river than it is to change the course of a discussion.

"Hawkeye is definitely *not* the smartest," I toss into the fray. Everyone nods. There is a moment of silence, due to the fact that my statement is immune to counterargument. I open my mouth to say something about the Decathlon, but before I can, Taniko jumps in to say that Loki's mastery of the art of dark sorcery is equivalent to Iron Man's education in mechanical engineering.

One of the facts of life at Howard Taft Middle School that you have to accept: the Whirlwind can get out a complete thought before you can finish your first word.

Finally, another moment of silence falls.

"Video Game Decathlon," I blurt out. "We should do it."

 "Oh, yeah. Right. We were going to talk about that," Peter says, as if he's waking up from an amnesia spell. "Josh is sick at sports games. So, back on?"

"Sure!" Taniko answers. Maya shrugs, but everyone seems to take it as a yes.

"So what should we call ourselves? I've already got a list of ideas!" Taniko asks as she pulls a page out of her notebook.

And of course she does. The Whirlwind is always one step ahead.

But none of Taniko's names are a big hit, and the debate begins.

Maya wants names that sound like cool bands no one has ever heard of, like The Vivid or Stalwart.

"Gloves Are Better," Peter suggests with a snicker. I clench my jaw and shake my head. I don't need Mittens any madder at me than he already is. Another fight and my mom will probably throw my video game systems into the city reservoir.

"If we're doing clothes, why not Socks with Sandals?" Taniko suggests, with a disapproving glance at Chen's feet.

"Link to the Internet," I throw out. I've always liked the puns in the titles of Zelda games.

Finally, with one minute left in the lunch period, we settle on a name that no one hates: The Tap Dancing Stormtroopers. It was actually the third name on Taniko's original list.

"Okay okay okay, but someone has to go sign up!" Taniko says as soon as the delicate negotiation is complete. Nothing gets the Whirlwind going more than a deadline, and teachers are starting to usher kids out of the cafeteria.

"Social studies always starts a couple minutes late. I'll take care of it," I offer.

I practically run to the office, hoping to sign up and make it back to class in time, but it turns out that we aren't the only group who are joining at the last minute. I have to stand in line, with time ticking down as other kids sign their names.

Finally I get to the front and am able to scrawl out our names. I'm a pretty good artist, but somehow that doesn't translate into good handwriting, especially when I'm rushed. And I butcher Taniko's last name. But I forget about that completely when I hear the voice behind me.

"Hurry it up, Creep." It's the sound of pure evil. My nemesis. Schmittendorf's voice has become almost painful to hear, like the screech of metal against metal.

I spin around, and he leans in to look at the list. "They decided to actually compete, huh?" His breath is rancid with sloppy joes from lunch, and I find myself wishing I could make a called shot to toss a breath mint into his maw.

I'd need to level up my throwing accuracy, though. And maybe learn a Conjure Breath Mint spell. I don't know of any magic shops in the area that sell that sort of thing.

"Yeah," I answer with a shrug.

"Don't forget I'm the champ, Creep. We're gonna annihilate you," he says. "I don't lose. Not to creeps like you. *At anything.*"

"Whatever, man," I say, stepping carefully around him and moving for the door.

"If you win by some cheat," he hisses as I walk out, "I will *end you.*"

The stench of the Mitten Monster's breath and the sound of his voice cling to me all day. I have to take a shower as soon as I get home from school. The last time I did that was when we had a straight-up food fight in fourth grade and I had tapioca pudding in my hair and turkey gravy in my ear.

# CHAPTER 8

## GOTTA CATCH...
## MOST OF 'EM

Despite the ravages of the Mitten Monster, when I wake up these days, I feel more than good. I'm alive again. I practically jump out of bed and put on my favorite shirt: Bilbo Baggins facing off against a giant-sized Yoshi in the Lonely Mountain.

By the time I'm walking through the doors at school, I'm mentally tallying up the experience points I'll award myself for successfully turning in all my homework and getting 9/10 on a social studies quiz. The chart hanging on my bedroom wall started out shaky, but now I have a chain of solid experience points earned every day for a couple weeks.

"Hey, Josh," Maya calls out, her backpack jangling as she jogs to catch up.

"Oh, hey," I answer, slowing to let her join me. Hearing my name in her voice leaves a flutter in my stomach—a little excited, and a little scared, too.

"So I heard something funny today," she says, and I know that it's not funny in a laughing way. She sounds concerned.

"What's that?" I say as we continue toward the busses.

"When I was in science doing a lab, I heard Henry Schmittendorf talk about how he scared you when you were signing up for the Decathlon."

I decide to play it cool.

"Not really," I say, giving an exaggerated shrug.

She steps in front of me, glaring. I stop short, staring into her eyes.

"Really? You're not scared of him? Not at all?"

I'm transfixed by her gaze. I don't think I can lie straight to her face.

"Well, of course I'm scared of him. He's like Bowser, but worse," I say, then sputter for a second, trying to figure out how to spin it. "But . . . but . . . I didn't show it! I'm not a total idiot!" If I can't be a tough guy, maybe I can settle for endearingly awkward?

Maya sighs and rolls her eyes. "Josh, this is serious. After that, he said, 'And by the Decathlon, the football season will be over. No games to miss if I get suspended.' Josh, I think he wants to fight you again."

"So? I'll beat him up again."

"Um, Josh . . . you realize I *saw* that fight, right? You have the combat readiness of a limp trout."

"Great metaphor," I say sarcastically. Ms. Pritchard forced us to spend a full class period coming up with metaphors the previous week. "But, you know, if you accelerate it to Mach 3, a trout to the face can actually be fatal."

She glares at me.

"Game, set, checkmate. The winner is . . . Josh Baxter!" I finish.

"You are so weird."

"A cool, sophisticated kind of weird," I say, pretending to be thoughtful.

"Sure, buddy. Whatever you say."

We walk silently for a few seconds.

"You know what the dumbest part of this whole thing is?" I say. "I actually *like* football. I used to play Madden all the time. If Mittens wasn't a massive jerk, I'd probably be going to the games and rooting for him."

"Really? You like football?" Maya raises an eyebrow. "Total weirdo," she says, as she steps onto her bus. But I think I catch a smile on her face as she disappears up the steps.

I mentally add a nice experience point bonus to throw on the board tonight. Maybe not a touchdown, but definitely a field goal or a safety.

"I saw you with that girl again." Lindsay practically pounces on me when I walk in the door. Leave it to Lindsay to be looking out the window of the high school bus while Maya and I were talking.

"Huh? Oh, Maya?" I answer. Playing dumb, because I can already tell where she's going with this, and I definitely don't need my sister blabbing about my "cute puppy love" to anyone who will listen, like she did when I had a crush on Tanya Phillips in second grade.

Lindsay smiles at me. The evil smile of someone who knows that she's right, even if you won't admit it.

"So you're going to ask her to the holiday dance, right?" She punches me lightly on the arm. She can see how uncomfortable this is making me. And she loves it.

"Uh . . . I don't know," I stutter. I can't fathom why she's interested in this. I certainly don't care what boy she has a crush on!

"You have to do it, Josh. Don't you get it? Girls *want* to be asked out. And Maya wants you to ask her out. I can see it in her body language."

"Huh?" I've heard the phrase before, but always in terms of being confident or scared or whatever. Can you talk with how you move? "Are you some kind of psychic, who can read people's thoughts from looking at them?" I ask. It actually seems like a pretty sweet superpower to have.

 "Ugh, Josh, you are such a weirdo. But— yeah, basically. That's how it works."

Whoa. My sister is, like, an oracle or something.

"Well . . ." I consider the situation. "If she's interested, why doesn't she ask me out?"

Lindsay throws her hands up in exasperation. "Because she's probably shy, dummy. Look, it's fine for a girl to ask a boy out. I've done it before. But it's hard. And she'll be much more impressed with you if you do it."

"She's shy?" That's not really the Maya I know. "She doesn't seem—"

"Dude, everybody is shy when they're asking someone out for the first time. Do you, like, know *anything* about love?" she asks, her blond hair waving as she shakes her head.

Once she's planted the idea in my head, I can't shake it. Can I ask Maya out? Is she really interested in me? The thought stalks me all through the next day, making it impossible to concentrate on my schoolwork. Mr. Ramirez could be giving out the winning lottery numbers in the middle of math class, and I'd probably ignore him and be stuck in school forever while other kids spend the rest of their lives riding Jet Skis in the Bahamas.

This whole "body language" thing seems pretty cool, but trusting Lindsay has gotten me into trouble before. Ever since the "habanero chili pepper incident"—when she said it would be fine and I ended up downing an entire carton of milk in seven seconds to try to counteract the unholy fireball that erupted in my mouth—I've been cautious about following her advice.

On the other hand, her social life is certainly worlds better than mine. But even if I choose to believe her, that doesn't help with the fact that thinking about asking Maya out terrifies me. It makes me want to grow a massive beard, flee into the mountains, and spend the rest of my life talking to no one but the mountain goats. So yeah, it's a pretty scary prospect.

My feeling of dread gets worse at lunch when I'm explaining to Chen my system for judging how hard to drift around corners in Mario Kart, and he stares off into the distance and changes the topic completely.

"Should I ask Taniko to the holiday dance?" he says, without any sort of introduction or transition.

"Uh . . . do you want to?" This would be a much better job for my sister, the Oracle. I'm too busy with my own thoughts about asking Maya to really focus on him, but I try to rein it in.

"Well yeah, of course," he says. "But I don't think my parents will let me."

"What? Why not?"

"My dad." He shrugs, like that ends the subject.

"Okay . . . what's his big issue?"

"He's super traditional. My mom's family have been here for, like, a billion generations, but my dad *really* wants me to date a Chinese girl. It's not up for debate with him."

"Okay. Well, what do you want to do?"

He shakes his head and looks totally defeated. I feel kind of bad. I'm having all this trouble facing my quest of asking Maya out, and because of his parents, Chen isn't even allowed to try.

"Can you talk to them?" I ask. "Tell them how you feel? It's the modern world now. Things have changed."

Chen shrugs and looks away. "Nah, man. Not worth it. Anyway . . ." He glances meaningfully behind me, where Taniko and Maya are approaching the table.

"Oh my gosh, Maya, you have to go watch the trailer," Taniko is saying as she sits down. "The bunnies will be able to build spaceships and fly them to other planets! We should put space bunnies in *our* game!"

*Our* game? I have no idea what that's supposed to mean.

Having friends is great—but some days it's also pretty weird.

At the beginning of the year, Ms. Pritchard stood in front of the class and said that we "can make whatever thesis statement you want in your essays, as long as you support it with evidence." I took this as a gauntlet thrown down, a personal quest for me to make the most insane thesis statement possible and then back it up with some sort of argument.

For my latest essay, I claimed that the lunch ladies served human meat on Sloppy Joe Fridays. And believe me, I have *piles* of evidence to prove my point, starting with the fact that I've never once seen a lunch lady or teacher eat cafeteria food. And they don't have Sloppy Joe Fridays in the summer, which is precisely when they don't have any students around to cannibalize! It all makes sense.

One of my favorite things about having Maya as a writing tutor is that, along with the many corrections and suggestions, she'll put a little smiley face next to the bits that she thought were cool or funny. And when we meet every week, she'll laugh at the ridiculous things I put in my essays and stories. It makes sitting at home doing my English homework a lot more tolerable, knowing that I'll get to see her reaction to them.

Monday has rolled around and she's helping with my Sloppy Joe Friday exposé, and we're laughing about how the grouchy guy at the cash register tells you to "have a nice lunch," as if you're a criminal headed straight to the gallows.

"Josh, you've really come so far."

"Thanks," I say, hoping my face isn't glowing the way my insides are. I feel like grabbing the essay and holding it over my head, like when Link finds a new key or sword in Legend of Zelda.

"Your writing is better, your ideas are clearer, and every essay or story is hilarious."

I nod, uncomfortable. I've never been good with praise. "Wow, thanks," is all I can say.

"I want you to know I'm really proud of you." She's

smiling at me almost sadly, and I'm confused as Ms. Pritchard walks over and sits down next to us.

"Josh, Maya tells me you've been doing exemplary work." She smiles at me, too, but hers is much more genuine and happy. "The stories you've turned in are tremendously vivacious. They're always . . . so whimsical."

I continue nodding, a little stunned by all the compliments. And in my experience, people being this nice almost always means that something bad is going to follow. I don't have to wait long.

"Because you've made such stellar progress, you no longer need a tutor. We have another student who needs Maya's help now."

"But . . ." I start to object. But I can't think of any reason. I know my writing isn't amazing—it's nowhere near as good as the piece of Maya's that was in the school newspaper, for instance—but I'm doing fine. I don't really need special help anymore.

They're both watching me, waiting for a response.

I shrug. "It's been really great, Maya," I say. "Thanks for your help."

She smiles at me for real, and somehow my head fills with joy while my heart feels like it's being crushed. It reminds me of the first time Lindsay and I laughed about something after Dad was gone. It felt amazing, and at the same time like a horrible betrayal. The thought that November is just around the corner slams into me, and I can't quite breathe.

I have to get out of there before the air chokes me. I try to give the Enchantress and the Punk Princess a serious look as I croak out a "thanks again, see you tomorrow" and grab my backpack, almost running for the door.

On Tuesday our midquarter reports come out, and the news is not good. The Wall of Heroes is going to be sad tonight.

My work has paid off in English, social studies, and science, but in math I seem to be losing battle after battle. Despite technically doing the homework and marking it down as experience points. But math was the worst early on, and I have a lot of ground to make up. I've been training, but in the last couple tests that Gym Leader Ramirez has thrown at me, I haven't done much to counterbalance the earlier grades.

Which is another way of saying that "practicing" for the Decathlon has meant I haven't exactly been focusing on putting one hundred percent effort into my homework.

To my credit, I don't shrink away from it this time. I walk straight into the living room and hand Mom the midquarter report. Well, as soon as she's gotten home, changed into comfortable clothes, eaten, and landed on the couch to watch her favorite British comedies. I wait upstairs to hear her signature hooting laughter to make sure she's in a good mood before I head down to face my fate in the Queen's Hall of Justice. She's going to get an email with it tomorrow, anyway.

After the drop-off I try to casually keep walking, heading straight up the stairs.

"Josh, come back here," she says, sounding incredibly tired.

This is one of those battles where the doors close as soon as you walk in and won't open until the showdown is over. She pauses the show and rests her chin in the palm of her hand for a few seconds before saying anything.

"You're on track for a C-minus in math? Really?" she finally says. "And Mr. . . . Ramirez . . . has a note saying your work at home could use improvement. It's this Decathlon thing, isn't it?"

I shrug. I'm not going to lie to her, but I won't make it easier, either.

She sighs. "This isn't just a little thing. Math is *important*. You're the son of an accountant and a financial manager; you should know this! And your sister is in the advanced track."

I look at the floor, drawing invisible lines along the creases in the carpet. Does she think I don't know how easy this stuff is for my sister?

"Look, I know it's important to do this competition with your friends. I'm not going to say you can't go and play with them, or participate in the Decathlon. But no more practicing at home all night long. I'm going to have to take your systems away again."

"Really? But . . . I did so much! I got my grades up in everything else," I protest.

She looks me squarely in the eye. "If the games are getting in the way of you getting your work done and getting decent grades, then you can't play them."

I stand there fuming for a second. Then I can't hold it in any longer. "They have a totally different setup here. And they did at each of the last two schools. I do the work, but half the time I don't even know what the book is talking about."

Mom winces, but a moment later returns to her firm tone. "And when you run into those problems in the homework, do you deal with them? Do you look them up, figure them out, ask for help?"

"Okay, I get it," I growl.

"Josh," Mom says.

"I'm sorry," I answer, trying to mask the anger in my tone.

"It's okay, Joshie," she says, shaking her head. "I know you're upset. I'm sure you'll do the work to get them back up. I believe in you."

I nod, super quickly, not looking at her, and climb the stairs. As soon as I'm back in my room, I flop down on the bed.

It's like those games where you think you've won, and then find out that you have to play through another entire level, where all the same enemies come back twice as big and three times as angry. Only without the fun of it actually being a game.

And it's not fair. I worked so hard! I can see the experience chart hanging on my wall, covered in the marks to prove it. Isn't that enough? What more can the universe demand of me?

I sit there, pondering my failure. Downstairs, life continues on as Lindsay gets home from volleyball and Mom bangs the refrigerator to stop it from buzzing.

Mom's right, of course. I've been skipping over the hard bits, and not stopping to figure things out. I've been treating the math work like something I just needed to show up for, and not engage in. Somehow I don't think Gym Leader Ramirez would approve of that strategy. It's like going into a major battle with a new Pokémon without bothering to evolve it. If I'm playing to win, I need to get serious.

As the Decathlon gets closer, I start spending more time at Peter's house, practicing. Since I'm not allowed to play games at home, it's really the only option.

So the Carpeted Dungeon is rapidly becoming my second home. Home is where the games are, after all.

"Peter, stop messing around!" Maya says, punching the couch in frustration.

Peter is playing as Link, bouncing around shooting his bow at us. Maya and Peter are up against me and a computer player, and Maya is getting more annoyed with every arrow.

"I'm unstoppable!" Peter says gleefully. "You've been knocked off twice, and I've barely been hit!"

Of course he hasn't mentioned that I'm the one who actually got the knockouts. I keep quietly fighting Maya's Bowser with my Yoshi, easily avoiding Peter's arrows.

Maya scowls. "You're not getting hit because you're not doing anything! You run away from everything. We're supposed to be *practicing* here."

Peter shrugs. "You and Josh are going to win Smash Bros. easily. It will be no contest. Let's just have fun."

"Probably, but we can't practice if you won't take this seriously! You know Zelda is my favorite game; I'd love to sit around and do nothing but that, but it wouldn't get us anywhere."

Peter grunts. "Come on, Maya, you always try to take something fun and make it into work." Taking things seriously isn't the Rogue's strong suit.

I sigh. "Guys, can we play the game?"

Peter grins. "See? Josh agrees with me!"

"No," I stuttered, "that's not what I—"

"Okay, Peter, if you want to lose your matches that's fine by me," Maya says. Somehow I doubt her sincerity. "I'm not going to be embarrassed by you."

Peter opens his mouth to make a retort, but instead his mom's voice comes from upstairs, calling his name.

"Oh, no," he grumbles. "My grandma was going to call tonight. She wants to practice her English, which basically means asking me what I ate for every meal the last week and how the weather is. She thinks if she learns English she'll meet a rich American man who will buy her a house with a pool. I have to go for a bit."

"Good luck," I say. "Tell her you went vegan and it's raining actual cats and dogs."

Maya doesn't say anything, just takes my momentary distraction to knock Yoshi into the abyss and win the match.

"Okay, let's do this for real," she says, tapping in the settings for a team match with the two of us against three computer players.

We play in silence for a few minutes, apart from the occasional "look out" or "get up there," until it becomes clear that we aren't going to win.

Distantly, we can hear Peter speaking slowly at the top of his lungs. "YOU'RE RIGHT, IT'S GETTING COLD HERE, GRANDMA. YES, I STILL HAVE THE SCARF YOU KNITTED ME. IT'S . . . VERY PURPLE."

I mount a desperate last minute gambit to lure the enemies into a trap. Maya is already out.

"So, Josh," she says.

"Yeah?"

"You going to the holiday dance?"

"Yeah. Maybe. I hadn't really thought about it," I say. Which is, of course, a complete lie.

She nods, watching my character get trashed on the screen. My hands are sweaty, and the controls are slippery under my fingers.

"Is it like . . . do you usually have to go with someone?" I ask. "At my old school everyone kind of went to dances and milled around, trying not to make eye contact."

Maya bursts into laughter, and I chuckle along nervously. "Yeah, it was like that here, too. My eighth-grade friends from writing class tell me it's different now."

In my chest, my heart is about to either go supernova or collapse into a neutron star. Is she hinting at something? Or asking for advice, like Chen? I wish I had Lindsay on a radio implanted in my ear telling me what to do.

"What about you?" I hazard.

She shrugs. "I don't know. I guess I'm hoping someone will ask me. We'll see."

Who is she talking about? Could it be me?

"Are you thinking of asking anyone, Josh?" she asks.

"I, uh . . . haven't really thought about it," I say. Which is not true at all. But it's all I can come up with. "I don't really know anyone all that well."

"Isn't that the point, though? To get to know someone?" she asks.

Before we can say anything else, Peter comes stomping down the stairs, loudly complaining about his grandmother.

"Really, Peter, I'm sure she's a nice old lady," Maya scolds him.

"Yeah, a nice old lady on the prowl," he grumbles. "She asked me where I think older bachelors hang out!"

We all start laughing and it falls into place: Peter. He must be the guy she's hoping will ask her to the dance. I might think they argue too much, but isn't that a thing? People who like each other argue a lot?

I keep turning it over in my head the rest of the night. In bed, I lie awake wondering how my council of heroes would handle this situation.

## ARAGORN FROM LORD OF THE RINGS

would have lots of longing looks with the person who might or might not be interested in him. But he'd never do anything about it, because of honor or whatever.

*Strategic Assessment: This seems like a wildly ineffective strategy. And yet it appears to be my go-to move. I really don't want to be one of those heroes who can defeat an army of bloodsucking spiders but runs away the first time he has to express his feelings.*

## FINN FROM ADVENTURE TIME seems likely to

actually do something about his feelings, even if it doesn't work out perfectly. And, unlike most adventure heroes, he's had a couple girlfriends. Finn would probably freak out about it for a day, then go right up to the girl and go for it.

*Strategic Assessment: Finn is a bold adventurer, but he'd blunder in and do exactly the wrong thing. Though Jake usually tells him in advance that his plan is a bad idea. Unfortunately, I spent years asking my parents for a dog and never got a normal one, let alone a magical stretchy yellow one.*

The next day, in honor of Jake (and to try to capture some of his ridiculous charisma), I wear my favorite T-shirt. It has Jake from *Adventure Time* taking the shape of Pikachu while Finn yells, "Jake-achu, I choose you!"

It's not my proudest moment, but I wait at my locker until Maya shows up. I figure if I don't do something now, I'll lose my nerve. All night I've been playing the scenario in my head. How smooth I'll be, how easy it will be to get the truth out in the open. And I might even get a date. It all makes perfect sense in my head.

When she shows up, I make it look like I'm finishing up packing for my first class.

"Hey, Maya," I say.

"Hey, Josh," she answers. Alarms go off in my head. *How* had I thought this was a good idea? It's like trying to scale the Peaks of Social Skills armed only with a Grappling Hook of Awkwardness −2.

"About what we talked about last night," I start.

Maya looks at me expectantly.

I freeze. The Abyss of Not Knowing What to Say yawns below, with the promise of the Jagged Rocks of Looking Like an Idiot on either side.

I have a million thoughts dancing in my head. I had thought through a whole routine about how "I'm also into someone," and I would use subtle language and skillful interpretation of that "body language" stuff to make sure that I was on the right track. And I realize, right in that moment, that all my scenarios had ended in her basically asking me out.

Crud.

I try to come up with a next move, but it's like a northern troll shaman cast one of those ice spells on me.

She raises an eyebrow. I stand there, frozen in place.

The moment stretches on, ice spreading through my entire body down to the tips of my fingers. "You're a weirdo," she says with a disgusted sigh, and turns and walks down the hallway. The wind howls around the empty mountain slopes.

That night I go straight home and collapse into my bed. I feel completely worthless. It's like accidentally deleting a saved game—everything I've been working for is completely gone.

# CHAPTER COMPLETE

## LEVEL 3

### BACKPACK WANDERER

**HEALTH**

**NEW SKILLS UNLOCKED**

Smoothness of the Porcupine

Not the Sharpest Crayon in the Tool Shed

XP +3570

# CHAPTER
## 9

# THIS NEXT TEST IS IMPOSSIBLE

It's Tuesday after school and the five of us have planned to meet up for practice. The Rogue and the Punk Princess are already there, bickering about whether to play a game we all like ("But I'm totally in the mood for some Karting, Maya!") or the one we need more practice in ("Peter, you guys need to run your basketball plays or you'll get crushed!").

The Whirlwind is there, too, and seems to be trying to get them to stop fighting with bursts of extremely compressed language, while I'm using my phone to remind myself which football players are the ones you want to use in the latest Madden. For all my bluster about being good at these games, I haven't actually played most of the sports games in a long time.

Maya glances over at my phone. "Come on, Josh, you really don't have those memorized yet?"

I sigh. "My mom won't let me practice at home anymore. I got a bad progress report in math and she took all my systems again."

"That's nuts, man," Peter says. "Does she want you to grow up to be one of those losers with social skills and a tan? Unbelievable."

"But that was our edge!" Taniko seems legitimately freaked out, though she also freaked out when Mr. Alpert was wearing nonmatching socks this afternoon, so it's all relative with the Whirlwind. "Josh, you're supposed to be our sports game super secret weapon!"

I shrug. "I'll get in some games over here, and I'll have to hope I can surprise them with some plays I've been reading about online."

I see the disappointed looks on Maya and Taniko's faces, and feel even worse about it than I already do. Will they want me off the team?

"I'm sorry, guys, I really should have been keeping up." I have a vision of returning to my old life, heading home every day with no friends and no games. "It's just that I missed a bunch of stuff in the transfer from my old school," I end lamely. It's a weak excuse and I know it.

But Peter doesn't seem to care at all.

"Who cares?" he says. "Josh is going to destroy them all the same. He's going to humiliate Mittens!"

My stomach twists in on itself at the thought of going up against the Mitten Monster, especially without being properly practiced. I can already see his gloating face. Hopefully we won't be matched up.

"Peter, that's exactly the attitude that's going to make us lose!" Maya says, getting a little flushed.

Peter and Maya are really starting to get into it when Chen comes down the stairs with slow, plodding steps. We all, including even Taniko, fall silent by the time he gets to the bottom of the stairs. I'm not an expert body language oracle like Lindsay, but even I can see the utter desolation on his face.

"I'm sorry, guys." He stops at the bottom of the stairs and stands there. No one says anything for a long moment.

"Oh my gosh what happened?" Taniko finally bursts out, puncturing the silence.

Chen shakes his head. "My dad says that you guys are distracting me from doing my work. All because I got one A-minus, and . . . and also I think he just doesn't like you guys. It totally sucks. But I can't practice with you anymore, I can't be in the Decathlon, and I can't work on building our game, either."

I wonder whether this has something to do with our earlier conversation, but I don't say anything. I'm not a *complete* moron. And I'm not sure what game he's talking about building, but this doesn't seem like the time to ask.

"My mom said I could stop by and tell you," Chen continues. "She's waiting in the car outside. My dad doesn't even know I'm here—Mom said she won't tell him."

"And I thought I had it bad," I mutter.

"I'm sorry, man," Peter says, sounding sad for the first time I've seen yet. "What a pile of crap. That totally blows."

By the time Chen has climbed to the top of the stairs,

Maya is fuming. Her hands are clenched and her face is scrunched up. "I can't believe that. His dad is such a jerk."

"We should do something." Taniko jumps up and starts pacing around the room. "We have to do something. Sneak him out, talk to his dad, *something*."

Peter shrugs. "Not much we can do. In the end, Chen always does whatever his parents say. He's too scared to talk back to them. He just accepts it."

I stay quiet, not knowing what to say without revealing what I know. Did Chen really only confide in me? I guess it makes sense that he wouldn't want to tell Peter, who has a tendency to do whatever he thinks is best without regard for what other people think.

"I don't know, guys." Maya's voice is brimming with frustration. "I don't think we can do this. Josh can't practice his sports games; we needed Chen for Splatoon and Mario Kart. And *you* don't even care about practicing," Maya says with a glare at Peter. "Let's just quit it."

"Whatever," Peter says, as he switches off the game that we'd been playing. "You take it so freaking seriously that all the fun is sucked out of it. It's supposed to be about games and having a good time, not another thing to stress over. I get enough of that at school. Let's forget the whole thing."

"Are you guys sure? You really want to give up?" Taniko looks heartbroken.

I put my head in my hands. The anger in the room makes me feel encased in carbonite, unable to move or speak.

"Come on, Taniko, let's go work on our game design,"

Maya says as she pulls on her coat and grabs her bag. "We've been slacking off on it anyway. See you tomorrow, Josh." Maya throws a sad smile my way before stalking up the stairs.

"See ya," Taniko adds as she follows.

"Bye," I answer. My voice echoes through the empty basement.

"Okay, great," Peter says, his voice brimming with fake cheer. "Now that they're gone we can play something fun that's not on the stupid Decathlon list. Something with guns and rap music."

I don't really feel like playing, but I also don't want to be alone right now. So we spend the next hour and a half playing the violent games that my mom would never in a million years get me for Christmas. It doesn't help a lot.

Walking home that night as the sun sets and the sky goes dark, it feels like the lights are going out on my life, too. I tried so hard, and now all of my friends hate one another. All because I tried to get them to do the stupid Decathlon. What's it even going to be like now, with no Chen and with Peter and Maya at each other's throats? Do I even have friends, now that they no longer need me?

Almost every hour that week I start to remember the milestones. I can't stop thinking about them, each passing like a howling ghoul. And now I let them slide by, and don't appreciate them.

I'm supposed to withdraw us from the Decathlon since I was listed as the team contact, but I don't bother. I don't care. What does it matter if we're still on the list? I'll figure it out next week.

Thanksgiving break is here, and on Thursday I try not to look at the clock, but I can't help it. I stare at it when 1:42 hits.

That was the exact time Dad pulled the Christmas decorations out of the attic, so that Mom would be able to put them up over the weekend. He walked past me, breathing hard. Of course, I figured it was because he was climbing in and out of the attic and carrying heavy boxes. Maybe if I'd noticed, and said something . . .

He made it to the garage before he collapsed. We all heard the crash, and I remember Mom running past me faster than I've ever seen her move in my life. It wasn't fast enough.

Two years later, and we're sitting around another new Thanksgiving table, just the three of us. I've sometimes thought we should have bought a triangular table for the dining room, so we don't have that one side of the table empty for every single meal together.

Mom has cooked all the traditional Thanksgiving food. She tries to start a conversation a couple times, but we load up our plates with turkey, stuffing, and mashed potatoes in silence. I try not to look at them, and steadily eat. I'm not that hungry, but I don't know what else to do.

Finally we're done. Mom puts her fork down really deliberately.

"We made it another year," she says. "There wasn't much to give thanks for last year. But I want you kids to know that I'm so thankful you're still with me. I don't know how I would have gone on without you. I love you so much."

"Love you, too, Mom," we both mutter in response.

I look down at the final, sad pieces of turkey on my plate.

Two years ago, Mom forgot about the oven when the ambulance came. The heat stayed on the whole time we were at the hospital, and when we finally got home at 2:00 a.m., the turkey was a charred pile of ashes.

"I think we're going to have a good year," Mom says, brightening up a bit. "I can feel it."

"What? Really?" I ask. How could she say that at a time like this?

"Yes, really. Things are getting better for us."

"Maybe a bit," I answer. "But for how long? How soon before we have to move again? Before we have to go to a new school? Before you press 'reset' on our whole lives?"

"Josh!" Lindsay says. I don't care what she thinks.

"I don't think we're going to . . . I didn't want to . . ." Mom can't quite figure out how to respond. I keep going.

"Dad died, and everything fell apart." I can feel anger surging in me. "Everything we've done since then has been wrong."

"Josh," Mom says, her eyes pleading with me.

"It's been one disaster after another." The wave crests.

She looks at me, then finally stands up. "I'm going to go lie down for a bit. I'll clean this up and put it away later."

She walks out of the room, her steps thudding in a slow rhythm down the hall.

Lindsay and I sit in silence for several minutes, both picking at our food.

"Did you really have to do that?"

I look down at my plate. "Do what?"

"I know you're mad, but did you have to pick today to say it? Of all the days?"

"No, I didn't," I answer, hanging my head. "I just—I don't know."

Empty minutes pass. The sound of the neighbors talking and laughing as they get in the car to go to a movie filters through from outside.

"Do you think Thanksgiving is always going to be this sad?" Lindsay says in a tiny voice. "Will we ever get back to normal?"

"I dunno," I answer, staring at the empty side of the table.

Distantly, I can hear Mom's door slam shut.

"You're doing okay," I say, struggling for anything to fill the silence. "I mean, you have lots of friends and you're doing well in school. You had them even last spring, and everything was perfect as soon as you got here. Everything always works out for you. You don't have to struggle at all. It was almost like nothing ever happened . . . like you didn't . . ." I trail off, realizing what I'm saying and seeing the stricken look on her face. "I'm sorry, I was trying to make you feel better, and . . . and . . ."

Usually when I say something mean or jealous she freaks out at me, but she doesn't this time. By all rights she should yell something horrible and storm off, after what I said.

"Joshie," she says, "it's not like that. My friends—they don't understand at all. I don't think most of them even know. And they care about the stupidest things. I feel like half the time I'm faking it, pretending to laugh and smile while I'm still walking around with this hole in my chest."

"I'm sorry. Me, too," I whisper. "And a couple things got screwed up, and now the friends I was starting to have . . . they all quit on me."

I'm not sure she's really paying attention to me; she just continues. "And I can't tell any of them, because they'll freak out. I don't want to be the one who makes things sad all the time. So I pretend along, like it's all fine. And there's no one I can talk to. Not even Mom—you see how she gets." She gestures at Mom's room.

"Linds, you can talk to me," I say. She doesn't reply. "Look, I'm sorry. I was trying to say something nice. I just . . . you just seemed so strong. I spent all of last year playing games. I couldn't face doing anything else, and when I finally realized I wanted to, I didn't know how. I was jealous, I guess."

She smiles a bit.

I shake my head. "So yeah, you can talk to me. Because I'm obviously so good at making you feel better."

It's not really that funny, but we both start laughing.

"I know you didn't mean it," she says after a minute. "I've . . . I've been taking any excuse to get out of this house. Sometimes I hang out with girls who annoy me, to be somewhere else. Even if it's a new house, it's still got all our old stuff in it. It's still where Dad is supposed to be. He's supposed to be here. He's supposed to be here with us."

I blink. "He was the one who always told us family was supposed to stick together. Whenever you and I would fight, he'd make us say that. 'We're a family, and family stick together.' And then he's the one who didn't stick with us. And Mom—she's supposed to be the one supporting us."

"It's not his fault. But it's just the three of us now. And Mom . . ." She looks in the direction of Mom's closed door. "This isn't her fault. She lost something huge from her life. And she's been trying so hard to make this work. You think she wanted to move again? I mean, I didn't want to leave our last school, either. But down here was where she could get work."

"Yeah, but—"

"She's doing this alone"—Lindsay cuts me off—"she's trying to make this work."

I sit back in my chair. The Oracle is right, of course. Stupid Oracle, always knowing when I'm being an idiot. And having the nerve to point it out.

"I was a real jerk." The cold gravy is starting to solidify on my plate.

"Yeah, you were."

"But you're wrong about one thing." I look up at her, trying to fake a determination I don't quite feel. "She's not doing this alone."

I barely sleep that night. I toss and turn for hours, and eventually drift off for a couple hours, but wake up again around dawn. I get up and walk downstairs, as the first rays of sunlight pierce through the empty house, and a new conviction fills my tired body.

*If you have something hard to do, the best time to start is now.* That's what he always told me.

What does a hero do when the adventure gets tough? When it seems like no matter what you do, you can't win? It's simple: Work harder.
Learn new tactics.
Level up. Play to win.

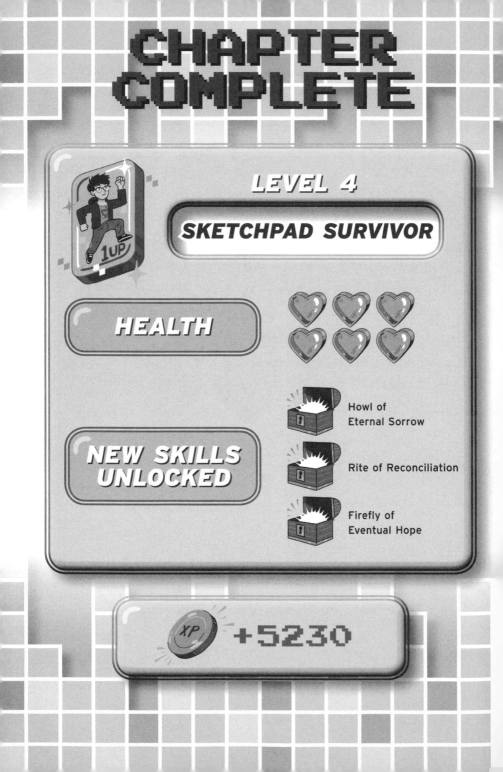

# CHAPTER 10

# PLAY TO WIN

I spend a lot of time over the weekend thinking about what I really want. There are a lot of things about my life that could be better, but I put four big ones on the Wall of Heroes:

1. *I need to fix my math grades and earn my games back.*
2. *I have to show Mom that I appreciate what she's doing for us.*
3. *I still want to complete in the Decathlon. Heck, I want to win it.*
4. *I want to ask Maya to the holiday dance.*

They're all pretty intimidating—to be honest, I don't really know how to start with any of them. Especially asking Maya out. As usual, I wonder what my heroes would do in my situation.

**<u>ASH KETCHUM</u>** would get over his fears and go for it.

**SOLID SNAKE** wouldn't be afraid, but would definitely go for it.

**HAN SOLO** would act like he didn't care, and then go for it anyway.

**SONIC THE HEDGEHOG** would already be a blurred streak of going for it by the time you even asked him.

**LINK** would travel back to the past and already have gone for it before you could even think of the idea of going for it.

> **Strategic Assessment:** *Every hero that I admire would double down and work twice as hard to bring his friends back together and go after the girl. Stop thinking about this and go get to work.*

I'm not ready to give up on my friends, and on the quest we started together. I want to compete, to put in a good showing, and most important, to do it with them.

Taniko seems like she'll be the easiest to convince, so on Monday I find her after math class.

"Hey," I say, and she looks up and smiles.

"Hey Josh what's up? How have you been? Did you have a good vacation?" Sometimes I wish I could record what she says with my phone and play it back at normal human speed.

I swallow. I hate asking for things, especially if it might make someone feel uncomfortable. But I've committed to doing this, in front of every hero I care about.

"The Decathlon," I force myself to say. "I think we should still do it."

"You know I want to," she answers, looking down at her notebook. "But we need Chen. And, honestly, Peter and Maya need to stop fighting. I can't deal with it. Too much stress."

I nod. "I know. But . . . if Chen would come back? If Peter and Maya could work it out?"

She shrugs. "If you can get them, sure. But it's not gonna happen."

I smile, trying to pretend I'm actually confident. "I think we can do it."

"Really?" She actually looks like she believes in me, which feels kind of weird and unfamiliar. "If you can pull it off, you know I'm in."

"Great," I say. I realize I'm sliding into manipulative territory here, but it's for a good cause, so I go for it. "Also, can you mention to Chen that you would be really impressed if he pushed back against his parents?"

Taniko laughs. "Josh, you're a bit diabolical. Okay, I'll try it."

"And one more thing," I say.

Taniko raises an eyebrow. "Sure, what's up?"

"Can you help me with the math test next week? I mean, really help me. There are a bunch of things that I really don't get. I think I missed a few units with all my moving last year."

"Of course I will! It will be fun! I'll bring my colored pens to draw you lots of diagrams!"

It's the first time in my life that I'll study for a math exam more than a day before the test. And I'm dreading it already.

Chen is the next stop on this quest line. I know there isn't much I can do without getting him on board. He and I have science together, which is right next to the cafeteria, so usually we get through the line together and almost always get to the table a few minutes before everyone else. Yesterday, Maya and Taniko went off to sit at another table. Things have been pretty chilly between Peter and Maya.

"So what gives with your dad?" I ask as the lunch lady drops burgers that are totally made from real beef on our plates.

"I dunno, he thinks my friends are distracting me from schoolwork. He doesn't want me to have a life. And he thinks video games are a waste of time." He shrugs, and we walk over to our usual table.

I have a suspicion. "Is that really it? That's the whole reason?"

"Okay, okay," Chen says, shaking his head. "They found . . . I wrote something stupid about Taniko in a notebook, and my dad happened to see it. And all he cares about is that she's not a 'nice Chinese girl.' Which is ridiculous, because he complains about racism all the time! But he also thinks I'm too young to hang out with girls. So he says I'm not supposed to hang out with her."

I sit back. I don't have an easy solution for this one. There's not some object I can fetch for him or monster I can defeat. Attacking his dad with lightning magic is not really a viable option.

He looks off into the distance for a long moment, and I wonder if I should leave.

But finally I see his jaw set, and he looks back at me. "I have to do something, or this crap will continue forever. I'll talk to my mom first, and see if she'll help me."

Peter joins us a minute later, but the girls don't show for a second day in a row. I do notice Taniko and Chen talking at Chen's locker at the end of the day. I look away and walk past like I'm late for something, afraid that Chen will see me and think that I sent her.

When we meet up to study after school that day, Taniko doesn't mention anything, and I don't ask her about it. No, there are plenty of distractions in the form of charts, graphs, and equations. She uses her fistful of pens to write the terms of equations in different colors, which is pretty clever. I'll have to see if Mom will buy some pens for me.

Taniko is a good teacher, and it almost makes math fun. Emphasis on the *almost*.

At 5:30 Mom picks me up. She has to go to her other job after, so this is probably the only time I'll have to talk to her alone for a couple days.

We need to talk, but it's hard to start. And that means the time has to be now.

"Mom," I say. It's not much, but it's something.

She glances over at me. "What's up, Josh?"

I stare out the window, imagining myself jumping and dodging through the landscape, and zip-lining down a long power line. "I'm sorry I blew up at you at Thanksgiving."

"It's okay, Josh, I know—"

"No," I interrupted her. "It's not. I know how hard you work. I know how hard these two years have been. I know you . . ." I choke on the words for a second. "I know how much you lost, too."

She doesn't say anything for a minute. We sit in silence as the car hums along the road.

"Josh, I'm so sorry," she finally says. "I know how hard this has been. New schools, new classes, new friends. So many times in just a couple years."

"It's okay. At least I've got some friends now. And I've been getting help for the next math test. Taniko talks a lot and has too many pens, but she's really smart."

I look over at Mom. Her lips are smiling, but she still looks sad.

"It's good you're catching up on your schoolwork. Taniko sounds like a nice girl."

I'm relieved that she's happier with me, but it's not enough.

I don't want to say anything. It would be a lot easier to let the moment last. But if you have something hard to do . . .

"Mom, I know the school stuff is important. But this Decathlon thing really matters to me. It's the quest that will make everyone friends again. That will give me friends in the first place."

She sighs. "I get it, Josh. I do. This may sound funny to you, but I know what it's like to be in a new town without any friends." She looks around at the buildings we're passing by.

"Oh," I say. I hadn't thought about it that way.

"If the Decathlon matters that much to you, then you can count on my support. And I'm sure your sister will want to see you and your friends win."

I sigh. "If I can convince them to do it."

"What? They backed out?"

I shrug and look back out at the sidewalks sliding by. "Yeah, but I have a plan. I'm going to get them back into it."

"I'm confident you can pull it off, too," Mom says, as we turn into the driveway and park. "When you put your mind to it, I'm always amazed at what you can do."

"Thanks, Mom," I say. We get out and walk to the front door. "One more thing."

"What's that, Joshie?"

"Don't you *dare* move us again!"

We both laugh, and she ruffles my hair. "Don't worry about that. We're doing well here. This is home now."

I stop for a second in the front hall while she goes in to grab a snack before heading to the cell phone store.

I guess this is home now, isn't it?

I don't have to wait long to find out the results of my "diabolical" machinations. Before science starts the next morning, Chen slides in next to me. I can't tell whether he's happy or sad; he's just kind of agitated. I turn and raise an eyebrow.

He sighs. "It started out okay, but when I pointed out that what he was doing to Taniko was the same as what people at his old company did to him . . . he kind of freaked out."

"I'm sorry," I say. "I shouldn't have pushed you."

Chen looks at me, slightly confused. "It's not your fault. I knew what I was doing." He shrugs. "And, I mean, after yelling for a while, he said I could do it. But not to complain to him when I get my heart broken. I felt really good after I told him—but I'm pretty sure my mom was the one who made him change his mind. She at least wants me to have friends."

"So you're back in?" I feel a little guilty for how happy

it makes me, when Chen is clearly dealing with some heavy family stuff. But I won't lie; I'm pretty pumped.

He nods. "Yeah, let's do it."

I go home that day still in shock that I actually got Chen to convince his parents to let him come back. And when I get home and go to drop my bag in my room, there's another surprise waiting for me. Sitting in the middle of my room is a pile of game systems, games, and cords—everything that Mom took away.

There's a sticky note on the side of one of the consoles. It says, *I know how much this Decathlon means to you. And your sister is very persuasive. I think she's going to be a politician someday. —Mom.*

By the next day I'm feeling pretty good, and it gets even better when Mr. Ramirez hands out our tests. I walk up to  the front of the room and sit down with what amounts to a Certificate of Awesome on my desk—an 87. The absolute minimum needed to get a B+!

It had taken some work to get the Whirlwind to slow down to my speed, but in the end, Taniko's multiple-pens method of teaching had gotten me a pretty solid grasp of the last section. My spider-sense tingles and I look up as the Mitten Monster returns to his seat at the back of the room, scowling like someone sniped his power-up.

"Not good?" his friend Stan asks.

"Whatever," Mittens answers. "At least I'm sure I did better than Creep."

"Man, if your grades slip too much—"

"I know," Mittens says, cutting him off, but keeping his voice low. "I won't be able to play in the next game. And my dad will go completely berserk. Even worse than last time. I can't believe Creep did that. He's such an idiot. And he probably knew what would happen the whole time."

Apparently Mittens has forgotten how I took the blame for the whole fight.

Peter leans over from his chair and looks at the test sitting on my desk.

"Hey, B-plus," he says, louder than he needs to. "That's actually pretty good, Bax!"

There's complete silence from behind us. I stare forward, wishing Peter didn't have a death wish, and didn't feel like he had to include me in it as well.

Mr. Ramirez says a few things about the night's homework and lets us go.

"Move, Creep," I hear as I stand up. Mittens pushes past me, and as I try to back up, my calves catch on the chair and I thump back down.

For the rest of the day and the next, every time I see Mittens he makes a point of walking as near as possible to me and muttering "Creep" in a low voice. In class, across the hall, in gym— it doesn't matter. It's like someone pushed his "hatred" slider up to maximum.

The continuing harassment from Mittens is frustrating, but I know I can't give up. An adventurer doesn't stop just because an entire school is making fun of him. The next challenge is to get Peter and Maya to join back in. I thought I'd done the hard work, but when I explain to Peter the next morning that Chen, Taniko, and I are all ready to go for it, he gives me a dull look.

"If Maya's going to be a tyrant about it, what's the point? I wasn't really having that much fun. If you want to play video games, you guys can just come over and hang out."

Maya has more or less the same reaction when I find a chance to talk to her in front of Vaults 151 and 153 between classes.

"Look, if Peter won't take it seriously, what's the point? We'll get crushed and then everyone will feel bad about it."

I realize this isn't going to be easy. I need help. I hate asking for it, but when I think about it, none of my heroes made it through their quests without having to call on some allies. Half of them are about a team that all work together. So I swallow my pride and go for it—I need the Oracle.

That night I find Lindsay while she's in the living room binge-watching some show about people making out in spaceships. I wait for the moment between when one of the episodes ends and the next automatically begins.

"Linds, thanks for talking to Mom," I say. "You didn't have to do that."

She shrugs. "It was no problem. Honestly, I'll look for

anything to talk about with Mom when she's driving me home from practice. If I don't distract her, she goes into auto-pilot talking about getting ready to look at colleges. That's, like, a century from now; I don't want to think about it."

I nod. "I understand. That must be hard." I wait a second, until the opening credits for the next episode start. "So . . . are you thinking about a big university or a small college?"

She throws a pillow at me. "Shut it, kid."

"Okay, okay," I say. "Um, actually, I was hoping you could help me with something."

She looks up at me while an opening montage shows hot people kissing and yelling at each other in all different parts of space. There are some explosions, too, but generally in the background. Now, I'm not against kissing, but I think they would need to put in some more laser-gun fights before I'll think about watching it.

"I need to figure out how to get two of my friends to stop fighting."

She hits "pause" and swings around to face me, eyes alight. "Oooh, fun. Let's figure this out."

I start by catching her up on what's going on, how the Punk Princess asked too much of us, and how the Rogue rebelled.

"Okay." Her legs automatically crisscross the way they do when she thinks hard. "The first thing you need to do is make both of them feel like they've won."

"What? How is that possible? My friends aren't idiots; they'll notice if I trick them," I object. The Oracle is smart, but I don't think even she is capable of that sort of sorcery.

"You don't have to give them the same thing," she answers. "You have to find something that Maya wants, and find a way to make it sound like a good idea to Peter. And the reverse for Peter."

"Oh."

"Anyway, this is about how they feel, not about stuff. So you have to make each of them feel valuable, like they bring something special to the table. What are their skills?"

We mull it over, and the outline of a plan starts to come together in my head. One so crazy, it just might work. Lindsay has a whole set of tricks for me to use. By the end of our conversation I can only conclude that the Oracle really knows how to deal with people. When she's president, I hope she'll appoint me the country's first Secretary of Video Games.

The next time I catch just Peter and Chen at lunch, I decide to try talking with Peter to get things back on course.

"So, we all actually want to do the Decathlon, right?" I begin.

"Yeah," Chen agrees. Lindsay said that having more than one person on your side was important.

Peter shrugs. "I already told you no, Bax. It's not going to be fun."

"I get that. If you can't cut loose and try stuff out, you don't have a good time." Trick number one: say what they feel back to them in different words so they feel understood.

The Rogue nods. "Yep."

"The thing is, what you do is useful. When you mess around, you find new ideas and make us think about the games in a different way. You're like the R&D group, like the top secret lab where they're inventing robots that will accidentally kill us all." That's trick number two: make him feel like what he does is valuable.

He grins. "Yeah, that's exactly it! Kill all humans, that's my long game."

We all laugh, and I lean forward to make the pitch.

"But Maya's important, too. She makes sure we work hard and get precise strategies for the final game." Trick number three: get him to see the other side as having value, too.

The Rogue sighs. "Yeah, that's fair. And I do want to win. I want to destroy Mittens."

"So what if we agree to mess around and experiment half the time, and get serious and play to win the rest of the time?" The closing argument: offer something that feels like it gives him a win.

"Right on," Chen says. He's sitting back in his chair with a look of shock.

"Start out wild and then get intense," Peter agrees. "I like it. She's really in for this?"

"Yeah," I answer. True, she hasn't exactly said that, but . . . close enough.

With the Punk Princess, I have to run the same thing more or less in reverse. I catch her when we're walking out of gym. Even though I have my arguments ready, I'm way more nervous for this one.

"Hey, how's it going?" I say.

She smiles. "Other than my algebra test this morning, everything's good."

"So, the Decathlon," I say. I have to cut to the point—I don't have much time.

"Look, we already talked about—"

"Hear me out," I say.

"Okay, fine," she says in a slightly annoyed voice. I gulp as I realize that, in my enthusiasm, I interrupted her kind of loudly.

"You feel like Peter is just goofing around, getting in the way of us winning because he wants to have fun." Trick number one. Understanding.

She cocks her head to the side. "Yeah, that's pretty much it."

"And you want us to work hard so that we can win. And we all, even Peter, want to win. That's why you've been working so hard, trying to keep us on track." Number two. Sense of value.

"Yeah!" she answers. "That's why I don't get it. Why won't he work hard like the rest of us?"

I bite my lip. It's time to go for it. "He's like the experimental lab. He messes around, but sometimes he comes up with a great idea or makes us see things differently. Like his Pokémon strategy of combining Belly Drum  to supercharge Aqua Jet for a high-risk attack that only works if they don't expect it. We never would have come up with it if he hadn't failed at it five times." Number three. Both sides.

Maya gives me a look. "You know, you're kind of good at this."

And now it's time to close the deal.

 "What if we split our time between playing for fun and exploration, and serious practice?"

"All right, Josh Baxter. If everyone else is in—let's do this."

On the walk over to Peter's house after school the next day, I feel a little like I've been dabbling in the Dark Arts. Everyone is there, and a day or two ago none of them wanted to be. I haven't lied or tricked anyone, exactly. On the other hand, last night I was able to give myself a *big* experience bonus on the Wall of Heroes. The Dark Arts do have their perks.

This social stuff is going to take some getting used to. I still feel like Professor Lupin or Obi-Wan would probably give me a lecture if they found out. On the other hand—it worked, right? Sometimes you have to be a tiny bit villainous to get things done.

Things don't go back to normal immediately. When we all get down into the basement, the Carpeted Dungeon is weirdly quiet. Usually everyone is making fun of everyone else, and arguing over what we should do first.

"What should we play?" Taniko asks, when no one moves to start anything.

No one says anything for a long moment. Someone has to do something, or all my hard work will fall apart.

"How about Mario Kart?" I suggest. "I'll sit out the first round." I'm pretty sure scientific studies have shown that no human can possibly not have fun while playing Mario Kart.

They drive in silence for the first lap. It's eerie, hearing the joysticks tapping back and forth. When they round the end of the first lap, Chen and Maya are in third and fourth place, trailing behind Taniko. Peter is leading up at the front. I glance over and see his face in fierce concentration, twisting his controller as he zooms around each turn.

I look back at the screen. Peter is about to go off a jump when a streak of green shoots out from Taniko.

Peter doesn't even have a chance to react. The shell slams into his kart.

"Nailed you!" Taniko yells as Peter's Metal Mario plummets into the abyss.

The silence stretches for a long second.

"Oh, I am *so* going to take you down," Peter finally fires back as Lakitu drops him on the track. He takes the opportunity to throw a pillow at Taniko, who squeals as she ducks it.

Everyone laughs at them, and I can feel the tension in the room dissolve. My team is back.

# CHAPTER
## 11

# WE'LL GO TO SOMEWHAT DISTANT LANDS

It's game day. If the movie trailer guy were narrating my life, his grizzled voice would be intoning how every day of my life has led up to this one moment. Preparing for the climactic battle that will shape my destiny.

And he would be right.

I'm wearing my favorite T-shirt: Link with Yoda perched on his back, and a speech bubble above Yoda saying, "There is no tri-force. There is only do or do not force."

I sit through my classes, barely able to pay attention. No one else seems as distracted, even the other kids who I know are competing. I guess they think it will be "fun." Which it will be. This is my chance to do something that matters with my new group of friends. The whole day I feel like I've guzzled three cups of the fancy coffee that Mom makes every morning. I'm totally on edge.

When Mom, Lindsay, and I get back to school that night, the school parking lot is almost full. The Decathlon's a fund-raiser for the class trip, and all of the student council I-need-to-get-into-honors-classes-for-high-school-or-my-life-is-over types have turned out, along with everyone who wants to play. Of course, it's nothing like the football game days when we've driven by and seen cars lining the sides of the street half a mile before and after.

The gym is packed. There is a line of TVs and game systems along one wall. On another is a big whiteboard with the team names written out, along with the schedules and a place for the final results.

Taniko wanted us all to dress the same, but that was too much trouble, so in the end we all settled on headbands like Solid Snake. People give us funny looks, but I think we look pretty awesome.

Mr. Ramirez somehow recruited Ms. Pritchard to help him, and they go around announcing that we're five minutes from starting. The team huddles together.

Peter grins. "I know you guys think I goof off a bit, but I'm excited."

"Thanks for agreeing to do this, guys," I say. "This has made coming to school here a lot more fun."

"Let's have a good time, and do our best," Chen adds.

"I'm so glad we're in this together!" That's Taniko, of course.

Maya looks around at the group with a serious expression on her face.

"Victory or death," she growls.

Everyone busts out laughing, and we all give Peter and

Taniko encouragement as they get ready to play Mario Tennis—against a group from the girls' tennis team.

"Wiggler's reach is unstoppable!" Peter shouts as he and Taniko crush the first set, using Peter's clever strategy of having Wiggler stand at the front of the net and use his reach to smack everything back. It's less funny five rounds later when the same two girls crush Peter and Chen in Splatoon.

When we rotate around to the Tetris station, I learn an important lesson about Taniko. The whole time she plays she's leaning forward, holding the controller in a death grip, and staring at the screen without blinking. The Tetris blocks are barely visible as she plays, just streaks of light flying down the screen.

"You know, I think the reason she talks that fast is that she *thinks* that fast," Peter says as the bricks dance in front of us.

Maya showboats in Pokémon, and Peter and I throw down in NBA 2K but lose in FIFA Soccer. Some tiny redheaded kid bowls a perfect game, and Chen's best effort isn't that close. I realize as the other boy finishes out his flawless frames that Chen is the only one of us who hasn't won at anything yet. When the final pins fall, he makes a face and crushes his empty soda cup, then jams it into the trash.

At the end of the next game, a familiar voice comes from behind us. "I don't know the first thing about how that Smack Brothers game works, but you two are like a typhoon partnered with a hurricane," Ms. Pritchard says. It's certainly true—Maya and I are embarrassingly good at Super Smash Bros.

I glance over at the scoreboard when we sit down. Most of the teams have pretty mixed records. I swallow hard. With only two events to go, there are only two teams in the running: Our team, the Tap-Dancing Stormtroopers, and Footballistics, the team featuring the Mitten Monster. It's a dead heat. And, somehow, after the upcoming Mario Kart game, football against the Footballistics is going to be our final event. I wouldn't be surprised if someone on the class committee arranged it that way for Schmittendorf.

Chen appears to be playing through pure rage, determined not to let this be his third loss of the night. And while Chen is a pretty sick driver, drifting around the tracks like a pro, the thing with Mario Kart is there's a lot of randomness. I check the scoreboard: The Footballistics have already won their seventh match of the Decathlon.

People are looking at the scoreboard, and a lot are coming over to watch us, knowing that the only way the final event will matter is if Chen wins. I can hear the crowd behind me starting to chatter.

By the end of the race, Chen is swaying side to side with each turn, like a little kid who hasn't yet figured out that tilting your body doesn't make the kart turn faster. Everyone in the crowd is yelling, but more from general excitement than caring one way or the other about the outcome.

But Maya, Taniko, Peter, and I are jumping up and down and shouting like crazy people.

In the final stretch, the other player draws a boost and pulls ahead. Chen only snags a stupid green shell. The four of us watching are completely deflated. But Taniko keeps yelling, so after a second the rest of us do, too.

Chen waits until the very final curve, pulling closer with every passing second. Finally, only a few seconds from the finish line, he lets loose. The girl dodges out of the way wildly, and the distraction is enough to let Chen hit a jump, drift around a turn, and pull across the finish line first.

We go nuts. It's by far the most exciting seventh-place finish I've ever seen. But all he needed was to come out ahead, and he's done it. The grin on his face when he turns around lights up the room.

We rush up, crowding around Chen.

"That was fantastic!"

"You're an ace, Chen, an ace!"

"Oh my gosh that was amazing I can barely breathe!"

The sigh of relief I let out lasts about a second before I feel the pressure bearing down. If Chen had lost, then my match would only be stressful because it's against Mittens. Instead, the fate of the whole team is riding on me.

"Okay, Josh," Maya says as we walk in a clump over to the Madden station for the football showdown. "You just have to win this and we take the whole Decathlon."

"Yeah." I swallow hard. "Yeah, I know."

"I know you can do this I know you can Josh go for it," Taniko adds, then takes a breath and slows down. "We believe in you."

"I love you either way, man," Chen says. "And hey, if you lose, then I'm still the big hero."

"Jerk," Taniko says, grinning as she punches him in the arm.

"The hopes and dreams of nerds everywhere are riding on you, dude," Peter says with a grin. "So it's not like there's pressure or anything."

That makes me laugh for a second, and I almost feel like I can do it. But their expectations are like a thousand tons of steel pressing down on my shoulders.

At least now I'm a player. What I do or don't do *matters*. I'm ready to face this.

As we reach the station, Mittens is already there, holding the controllers. He gives me a mocking smile, holding out mine.

I reach out to take it, and as he hands it over, he speaks quietly.

"I'm going to destroy you. I don't lose. And I *especially* don't lose at football."

I look him in the eye, ignoring the piece of gum that's been stuck to the underside of the controller and is now attached to my hand.

I look him straight in the eye. "Good luck, and have fun," I say. I calmly wipe the gum off my hand with a napkin, clean the controller, and sit down. Mr. Ramirez comes over, standing in between us like it's a boxing match.

"This game must be played properly," Mr. Ramirez says. "I believe this is the first time that the final two teams have competed together in the final match. Fascinating."

"For the Decathlon we were only playing to halftime," Ms. Pritchard says, "but since this is the deciding match, Mr. Ramirez suggests that we play the full game. Would that be okay for you?"

I shrug. Mittens nods, and I'm pretty sure I hear him mutter something to one of his friends about having more time to embarrass me. Of course, the teachers are busy explaining to the people watching that we're playing a full game, and don't notice.

We select our teams, and before I know it Mittens hits "start" and is kicking off. It's game on.

At first, no one is really paying much attention to us, other than the two teams and a couple of girls who have crushes on Mittens.

 "Crush the creep!" one of his football buddies walks over and starts yelling when Mittens scores the first touchdown.

"Yeah, show him how the real game is played!" another one shouts.

But when I make one back, the chattering in the crowd behind us stops.

As the score stays close and we hit halftime, people are actually starting to cheer for us. Peter comes up behind me, slaps me on the back, and hands me a soda. "I can't believe you're doing it!" he exclaims. "Beat him. The whole school is watching. He will absolutely flip."

"Yeah, no pressure," I grumble. "And no danger to my personal safety."

"You let me take care of that. Just play."

Before the second half starts, Mittens glares over at me. "I've been messing with you," he says, leering like a jackal. "Now I'm going to tear you apart."

I shrug. "So if you lose, you're going to say you played badly on purpose? I'm sure everyone will believe you." It feels great to talk back to him, but I can feel the controller shaking in my hands as I kick off to start the second half.

"Mittens can't miss!" a girl cheers, when he's ahead by eight points.

"Sweep out the creep!" someone yells, but a second later the lead is down to three points.

And as I close the gap, I can even hear a few other people cheering for me. I actually screw up and run the ball into a trap after I hear some voice I don't know yell "Go Josh," and actually sound like he means it. But I rally and make the first down.

I glance over and the Mitten Monster has a dark look on his face. Big veins are standing out on his neck, and it looks like he's about to snap his controller in two.

When I execute a tricky lateral play, he actually growls

like an angry bulldog. "What are you doing, Creep? That's not football. Stop cheating."

I bear down, but he's good. While he's playing a traditional conservative strategy, I'm sending my guys on crazy plays to sack his quarterback and intercept passes that would never work in real football, taking advantage of the  game system. The truth is, both methods work pretty well. And he seems to play even better when furious.

The crowd is going totally wild, shouting as I match him touchdown for touchdown and interception for interception. When I take the lead for the first time, I can hear my teammates being joined by a bunch of other kids in cheering. I glance back and see that everyone in the whole place has finished their games and come to watch our extended final. Even the teachers and Mr. Alpert are there. The Frost Giant clearly has the best view, towering over everyone. The teachers aren't cheering for either side, though Ms. Pritchard seems to be grinning despite herself.

But the next time I try one of my tricks, Mittens counters perfectly.

"That's enough of your crap, Creep," he hisses. "I've got you."

The crowd goes quiet as he scores a touchdown and a field goal, with only a couple minutes to go. I'm spooked.

He's figured out a bunch of my plays, and I basically have this last possession to score.

The crowd response is mixed as I scramble my team down the field. "Let's go Josh, let's go Josh, let's go Josh!" I can hear Taniko yelling over the crowd.

"Come on, Josh!" I hear one familiar voice. "You can do it!" comes another one, echoing from the back of the room. It's Lindsay and Mom. And in that moment, I feel like Dad's there, too. This is exactly the situation he would get into, and then come up with some crazy play to send me into the kitchen to wear his oversized dish gloves and scrub the casserole dish.

I get so close, and people can sense when I run up against a wall. Nothing I'm doing is working. And the clock counts down. I only have one play left. I have to choose: try for a field goal and send the game into overtime, or try one last play to take the win.

Football coaches and armchair quarterbacks will tell you that you *always* go for the field goal here. And I know that. Mittens, of course, knows football just as well as I do. And he has real experience. He's seen this situation from both sides, and you always go for the field goal.

I glance over at him. He's grinning. He knows the situation—if he can block the field goal, he'll win. If I make it, then the game will go into overtime and he'll have another chance to beat me. And he has been figuring out my plays, one by one. Everything I'm trying runs up against a counter. He's shutting me down, and I'm not really in great practice.

I set my team up for the field goal as the clock counts down. I can see him nodding out of the corner of my eye as he prepares to go all out for the block.

Then comes the snap, the lateral, the coverage, the pump fake, the handoff, and a bunch of football terms you might or might not know. The I-don't-know-football summary is this: When all the moves are done, my kicker is running into the end zone with the ball while Mittens is still trying to figure out what happened.

Touchdown. Game over. The kids behind me explode, and I can even hear the teachers cheering. Kids who've never  looked twice at me in the hallway are chanting my name. But others are yelling things like "cheater" and "that's not football!"

Mittens stands up slowly. His face is flushed as red as a stop sign.

I expect him to jump at me. I tense, ready for fists to fly. But he gives me a curt nod and puts the controller down.

Then I hear a deep voice roaring above the rest. "That's not how you play the game. That's a load of crap!"

Schmittendorf's dad is pushing his way through the crowd. The giant Mitten Monster glares at me, then at his son. It's like that moment at the end of what you thought was the final boss battle, when the wall collapses and there's an even bigger one waiting for you.

"This is not acceptable!" he growls.

"Dad, chill out," Mittens mutters, turning away.

"No, this is ridiculous. You're a football star. How could you lose to this twerp?" He glares at me. "And what was that, kid? Hacker tricks? Cheat codes?" The veins on Mr. Schmittendorf's neck stand out the same way his son's do, but even redder and darker.

"Dad, please. Stop," Mittens says a bit louder. A complete silence has fallen on the rest of the crowd.

"Are you really going to allow this?" The Massive Mitten Mammoth turns to Mr. Ramirez now. "That sort of play is allowed? From the kid who made us lose against Lancaster?"

Mittens grabs his dad by the arm. "Dad, *he won*. I lost. Get over it. Can't I lose at something, just once? Can't you let this one thing go?"

Father turns on son, a tornado of rage. "Don't tell me what to do! Be a loser, then. Just another loser. I always knew it. And now you're a loser who's going to walk home."

Mittens's dad stalks off, the crowd pulling back as he kicks a trash can, slams the gym door closed, and disappears into the night.

Silence reigns.

"Don't worry, Henry, I'll give you a ride home," the gentle voice of the Enchantress finally says.

"Thanks, Ms. Pritchard," Schmittendorf answers glumly.

The crowd stays nearly dead quiet.

"I'm sorry about that, Josh," Mittens says, staring at the ground. Finally, he looks up at me. "Good game. That was a clever play."

"It could have gone either way there. Good game," I reply, and stick my hand out to shake.

I'm worried I might end up with another blob of chewing gum, but I can handle it. This is a lesson my dad taught me, from the first time we were playing video games together, or knock hockey and foosball in our old basement. When you win, you don't gloat. When you lose, you don't sulk. You say "good game," shake hands, and move on to the next game. Or go do the dishes, if Dad suckered you in again.

We shake in the awkward hush, and he turns and disappears into the crowd.

"Thank you, everyone," Mr. Ramirez says loudly. "Congratulations to the Tap-Dancing Stormtroopers! That's it for the Decathlon."

"Enjoy the pizza that the PTA provided, and get home safe," Ms. Pritchard adds.

The pizza party is a blur. A lot of people congratulate us, but just as many are glaring at us. It's as if Mittens having his dad freak out is somehow my fault.

Finally, outside in the parking lot, I get a hug from each of my teammates. The whole experience has left me dizzy, like I've had a cartoon anvil dropped on my head.

"You guys were amazing," Maya says.

"So were you," Peter answers. "We were unstoppable."

"I'm so glad we did this," Chen adds. "The look on their faces—I had no idea I could be so happy."

Taniko's mouth is going up and down, but no words are coming out. I think she's trying to say things so fast that her brain has short-circuited her mouth and is casting her thoughts directly out into the ether at psychic frequencies.

"Guys, thanks for giving this a shot," I say, trying to pretend that my voice isn't a bit choked with emotions. "Mom, I guess we have to go now?"

"Hah!" she says. "After a victory like that? No way! How about instead, the Tap-Dancing Stormtroopers let me buy them all ice cream?"

There are exactly zero objections to her suggestion.

Ten minutes of complicated carpooling later, we're all sitting together in the ice cream shop. I order something with chocolate, chocolate chips, chocolate chunks, and chocolate sprinkles.

"Guys, that was an amazing night," Maya says, raising her organic grass-fed vanilla yogurt for a toast.

"Thanks for helping me stand up to my dad," Chen says as we clink ice cream glasses. "He's still barely talking to me, but he'll get over it."

"And we crushed Schmittendorf. I almost kind of feel bad for him," Peter says with a rogue's snicker.

"Yeah, the Mitten Monster has his own troubles, I guess," I say. "That doesn't excuse his being a jerk, though."

"Mitten Monster? Is that what you call him?" Maya asks.

"Yeah," I answer. "He's a giant mitten, and throws tiny mittens at you . . ." I realize that I'm reaching for my bag, and the notebook is halfway out. I freeze.

"What've you got there, Josh?" Peter asks. It's too late to back out now.

"Show the class," Maya says in a playful voice.

"Show it, show it!" Chen chants. They can sense my awkwardness and, like good friends, are piling on. I'll never understand why that's a thing, but it definitely is.

I reluctantly put the sketchbook on the table and flip through it, trying to mentally note which pages to make absolutely sure not to show them.

"Here," I say, laying it down open to a full-page sketch of the Mitten Monster in all his fingerless glory. "There he is, and there are the deadly mittens he throws at you."

"Who is that?" Taniko asks, peering at the page. "Is that . . . Peter?"

She's right. I forgot about that bit. A tiny Peter the Rogue is slashing at the Mitten Monster's quilted armor with a glowing magic axe.

Before I can react, Chen grabs the notebook.

"I've got to be in here somewhere," he says, furiously flipping through the pages. I lunge for it, nearly knocking over my ice cream, but Peter grabs my arms in a bear hug.

"There's Taniko and me," Maya says with a chortle. "We look cute!"

"Finally!" Chen adds, when he flips to a portrait of himself throwing a lightning bolt, with *The Mage* written under it in fancy letters.

Finally, on the last finished page, there's a picture of all of us together that I drew last night when I couldn't sleep.

"Oh my gosh guys, that is so very totally positively perfect!" Taniko squeals.

Peter leans forward, looking closer. "It actually kind of is. We'll have to rip out a bunch of the stuff in the game now . . ."

Chen shrugs. "That's just placeholders that I made. It's total junk. You know I'm really just the tester and animator. I can't draw."

I shake Peter off me, and he finally lets go and starts back in on his pineapple coconut sundae.

"What the heck are you guys talking about?" I demand.

"Your art," Chen says. "The video game we've been making. We'll have time to get back to it now that the Decathlon's over."

"We had kind of stalled, since all the art we made was kind of ugly," Maya interjects. "Didn't we mention it do you?"

"Not exactly," I answer.

"Well now you're going to do the art for it!" Taniko says.

"I am?"

"Um, only if you want to," Maya adds. "See, we couldn't agree on a theme, but this is perfect. It'll be at a school, and the Mitten Monster will be the final boss."

"Taniko and I are programming," Peter explains. "Maya is writing the script and doing the levels, and Chen is testing it and will be getting it out to the world. The basic gameplay is pretty much there."

"So are you in?" the Whirlwind demands. "You have to!"

I sit back in my seat. I remember hearing that they were working on something, but had no idea how serious they were. "That . . . that sounds awesome."

I watch in amazement as they throw out all kinds of terms I don't understand, figuring out what changes they'll have to make to integrate my art into the programming, writing, and level design.

I take a spoonful of my sundae. It tastes like victory. Delicious, gooey, chocolaty victory. The Wall of Heroes is going to get a big splash of green ink tonight.

# CHAPTER
# 12

# YOUR PRINCESS IS IN ANOTHER CLASSROOM

The more I actually try at my life, the more I realize how many excuses I was making. I was constantly rationalizing how to surrender before the fight even started. "It's too hard," I'd say, or "It will never work," or "They probably don't want to."

An adventurer doesn't make excuses. Sometimes we have to do things that scare us to prove that we can. Because your mind is lying to you, telling you to stay in your safe zone, to hide at home and not take up the quest.

 You have to pick up your gear, rally your allies, and get out on your journey.

That's what I find myself thinking, sitting in math class, watching Gym Leader Ramirez lecture about something that Taniko already showed me a few days ago, and wondering why I'm not living up to my own advice. It all sounds great in my head—but it's much harder to actually live it.

You see, to be the hero I set out to be, I have one final

challenge to overcome: I have to ask Maya out. The holiday dance is a week away.

But the questions dance around in my head anyway. What if she says no? What if she's already agreed to go with someone else? What if asking makes things awkward and ruins our friendship? What if she turns me down and the awkward tension messes up our whole group of friends?

During one of our Decathlon practice sessions, Maya told us that her favorite game of all time was *The Legend of Zelda: The Ocarina of Time*. What if I set up a whole performance around that? How could she say no?

I sketch it out in my graph paper notebook, hoping Mr. Ramirez won't walk by and notice that I'm not taking notes.

I'll get speakers so the soundtrack is playing in the background, slowly fading in until she realizes what it is. I can make a Link costume, or maybe at least a hat. I might look silly, but hey, that's always a risk.

I sketch it all out, with Peter, Chen, and Taniko playing other characters from Zelda, and a great speech about how I've learned so much from her, and how I would journey through castles and temples, back and forward through time, between worlds, or anywhere else for her.

I'll need to get them all to join in, like I did for the Decathlon. I can probably get Lindsay to help with the costumes. She's been making her own clothes for years, chopping up old stuff and sewing it back together to make something new.

It's a grand plan, and I need to call on every resource I have to make it happen in time for the dance.

I'm brought back to math class when Gym Leader Ramirez stands at the front of the room and starts calling out names, handing each of us our graded tests one by one.

"Josh Baxter," he says.

As I walk to the front of the room, my world narrows into cinema mode. This is the cut scene where my judgment comes down.

"It looks like you have reached your next evolution, Josh," Mr. Ramirez says quietly as he hands me my test.

I return to my seat, take a deep breath, and look down.

91/100.

An A-minus!

I close my eyes and let out a breath. Is it perfect? No. But I did it. I'm back in the game. The controller is in my hands now. I put the test into my notebook to review later. Taniko is out sick today, but she promised to go over the problems I missed. This time there won't be too many of them!

The bell rings, and we all stand up to leave. And then another miracle happens. Mittens walks right by me. No whispered taunts, no funny faces. A couple of his friends walk behind him. One of them looks at me oddly—not mocking or angry, just confused. For the past three months, not a day has gone by without at least a whispered "Creep."

But now, as far as Mittens is concerned, it seems I no longer exist. I can live with that.

I walk out of the class and head to my locker. I stand in front of Vault 151 for a moment, looking down at the mess of lines and shading in my sketchbook. I imagine what the Oracle would say about my plan. The truth is, I don't even need to ask her.

"Josh. That is a dumb idea," Lindsay would tell me, probably making that exasperated grunt she does whenever I suggest something. "An unbelievably dumb idea."

I glance down the hall and see Maya walking toward our lockers.

And I realize, those plans, those questions, they're all more excuses. Made-up reasons not to take on the challenge. It's like Dad always said. "Why not do it now?" he'd tell me. "Now is always the best time to do something hard."

I try to call back that feeling from last week, when we won the Decathlon. Nothing could stop me then. I'd hit a power-up and was charging through every obstacle.

"Hey, Maya," I say.

"Hi there, Howard Taft Middle School Video Game

Decathlon Champion," the Punk Princess answers, with a wide smile. "What's up?"

No grand romantic gestures or performances. No gimmicks.

I just ask her.

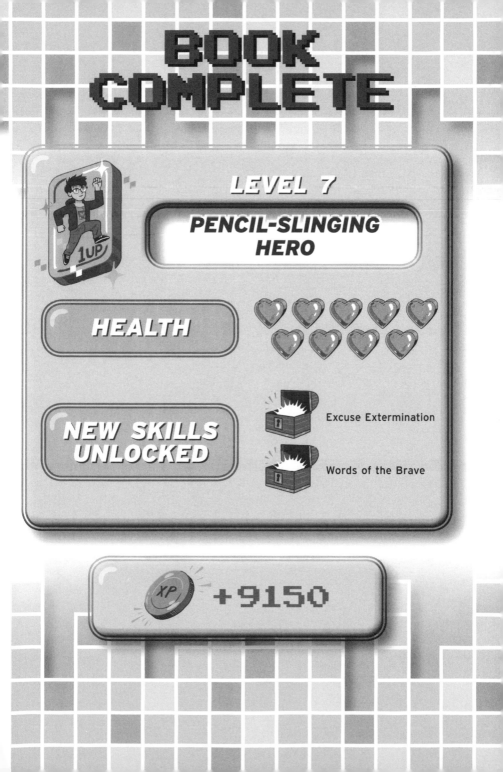

# Acknowledgments

Unlocking "book published" is a massively multiplayer achievement. Both this novel and I owe a great debt to Sarah Evans, who first hatched the plot to create this book and followed through with editorial expertise, creativity, and patience. Chris Danger's art and Christopher Stengel's design direction brought not just the cover but many of the pages to life.

The rest of the Scholastic team, including production editor Emily Cullings; copy editor Daniel Letchworth; proofreaders Gabriel Rumbaut, Maya Frank-Levine, and Lindsay Walter-Greaney; and Kirk Howle and Joanna Gras in manufacturing, were all vital in bringing this book to its final form. I would also like to acknowledge Ellie Berger, Lori Benton, Nelson Gomez, David Levithan, and Abby McAden for their support of this amazing opportunity, and Rachel Griffiths for giving me my first shot at getting published just a few years ago. In addition, the teams all across Scholastic Trade, Book Clubs, and Book Fairs have been incredible both for believing in this project and helping make it a reality.

In the world outside of Scholastic, I would like to thank Ash Byrnes, Carrie Brown, and Keith Fretz for reading versions of this manuscript, as well as Grace Kendall, Laura and Michael Bisberg, Laura Jean Ridge, and Nick Eliopulos for their feedback on its early stages. There are pieces of your inspiration and imagination throughout. And I must especially thank Mallory Kass—you built me up and have had the generosity not to destroy me.

To my many friends and family members, in New York and spread across the world, thank you for sharing your lives, your wisdom, and your laughter. And finally, to my nuclear family Yorke, Carrie, Galen, and Christine: thank you for being my fusion-powered core.

Thank you all for joining my adventuring party on the journey that led to *Josh Baxter Levels Up*. Say the word and I'll unlock my vault, grab my gear, and ride out to join your quests.

This concludes my emotions. Please turn the page to enjoy my biography and a moderately smug photo.

# About the Author

*Author photo by Michael Bisberg*

**Gavin Brown** has written stories and designed games for the bestselling Spirit Animals and The 39 Clues series, and is the creator of the highly rated iOS and Android game Blindscape. He lives in a narrow apartment in New York City's East Village.

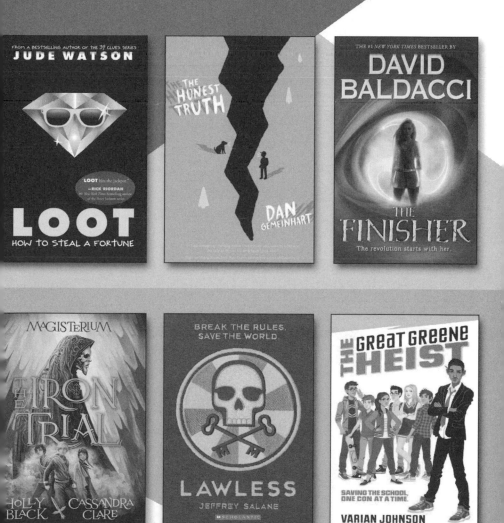

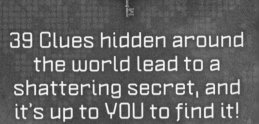
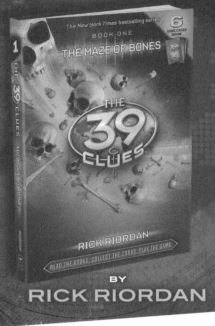